IN THE WORLD OF HYBORIA

By

Lawrence BoarerPitchford

I0626369

In the World of Hyboria: Book 1 Grim Determination; Book 2 The Ties that Bind

Lawrence BoarerPitchford

Published by Lawrence BoarerPitchford, 2022.

IN THE WORLD OF HYBORIA: BOOK 1GRIM DETERMINATION; BOOK 2 THE TIES THAT BIND

First edition. February 17, 2022.

Copyright © 2022 Lawrence BoarerPitchford.

ISBN: 978-1736509654

Written by Lawrence BoarerPitchford.

Table of Contents

DEDICATION

This one is for all the Robert E. Howard fans out there.

ACKNOWLEDGMENTS

Thanks to all who have supported me in my effort to bring these bawdy action stories to life.
Cover Artist ~ Lawrence BoarerPitchford
Editors ~ Julie BoarerPitchford
And
David Perrault

BOOK 1
Grim Determination

CHAPTER 1
A Sticky Wicket

THE STENCH OF URINE filled the air, and the reek of animal dung assaulted the average passerby with a sticky acrid taste. A monkey on a chain jumped out and held up a small brass cup. "Be gone wretched creature," Benhargan chided as he stepped over the beast. The end of his scabbard struck the monkey on the head and the creature let out a wail then ran to its master. The monkey's owner wisely kept his mouth shut.

Benhargan's shoulders sailed above the heads of the Khemi residents. They looked upon him as a freak, a strange anomaly of creation too large to fully comprehend. His size and language made him stand out, in a place where standing out was dangerous. Stopping at a dark doorway he reached for the wooden latch, flipped it up and opened the door. Inside a cacophony of voices blasted his ears. Men shouted while throwing dice and argued bitterly afterward. A woman screamed angrily then laughed with bawdy guffaws. Men were nearly shoulder to shoulder, and Benhargan cut through them like a ship's prow through blue waters.

A swarthy fellow, like most in the tavern, approached Benhargan. In his hand was a bundle of brown linen containing something. The man stopped nearby and looked at him. With his hand the man motioned for Benhargan to come over.

Benhargan pushed his way through the throng and stopped at the narrow rough fashioned table. "What is it?"

"Oh, great fighter, it is something you've been asking for."

"If you want to see my brass, you'd better be quick about it."

The man looked around then unwrapped the item. A small urn appeared, dusty, encrusted with filth. The fellow dusted it off then smiled a toothless grin, "You see, it is just as I told."

A patron bumped against Benhargan and Benhargan moved faster than most could see. A scream filled the air and blood spurted at him and onto the table. The swarthy fellow's eyes went wide as Benhargan placed a severed hand on the table. He made no facial expression, "As you were saying."

"Whose hand is that?" The Khemite said fear hanging on each word.

"It is unwise for a fool to loot the purse of a man such as I. He will be easy to find once our business here is done," he nodded into the crowd and the bloody trail through the tavern. "Now listen well. I'm here in your foul land for far too long, and by Crom if you keep me here wanting more, I'll have your eyes for it," Benhargan said.

"I swear it, the container holds the item you seek."

Benhargan took the item and with his brute strength ripped open the top. He angled a candle over the opening. For a moment he stared inside the jar, a dull yellow reflection of the candle shimmering across his hairless face. "This will do," he said, stood up, tossed five brass ingots on the table and pushed his way through the crowd toward the door. Looking down the dark stain of blood ended at the portal; he opened it, and the trail began anew.

He followed the trail to an alley where the dark blood vanished into an even darker shadow of the passage. He knew better than to go in there. An enemy could be around any doorway, or waiting above in an open window, ready to club or stab him, or worse. The thief would have one more time to lose his life as Benhargan would not be killing him today.

Walking on he came to a caravan preparing to depart into the desert. From there, he turned and walked down to the marina. His task was done for now, he'd secured the relic and now would return it to his employer. But he had one more stop to make; a friend to fetch from the torture pits of Taraturn. A friend who saved his life, and he hated him for it. A man whose name struck fear in the hearts of Picts, Hikarian bushman, and whores alike: Bulvife.

BENHARGAN LOOKED OUT over the railing. The ship gently pitched from side to side. The seas were mostly calm, but for the constant roll of the blue waves. "Here is fine," he said and climbed down into a small rowboat. The coast was like much of the country of Tara, bleak, dark and rocky. Even the city, hewn from white marble and gray limestone was as void of cheer as its land. He took up the oars, cut the rope and began rowing toward a particularly jagged group of black rocks.

"Good luck Cimmerian," called one of the sailors. "We'll be waiting here until night fall. Then it's too dangerous to be out on the sea; the beasts will wreck the ship and devour those who touch the waters."

Glancing back Benhargan grunted and pulled at the oars with such ferocity that the three-inch-thick wooden rods bent like ballista bows. The boat picked up speed, and soon was careening through the razor-sharp rocks and over the jagged coral. Every few strokes he looked over his shoulder, angling the boat towards a fissure in the high cliff face.

He raised the oars and stowed them allowing the boat to glide into the shattered shore and wedge between two large rocks textured like metal files. The wood shaved from the sides and the boat stuck tight. He climbed onto the rock and slowly upward.

He climbed hand over hand finding foot holds where only imagination allowed them to exist. Birds angrily chided him, and more than once he placed his hands in guano, white and freshly placed by the offended. At last, he reached up into the fissure and a stout and foul wind blew back his dark hair. "Lord Crom's hairy ars," he said as he rolled up and into the hole. "The stench, by Crom the stench."

For a moment he tried to recover his breath to no avail. It was as if the air of the cave stole his wind from him. He struggled to his feet and looked down. Dark shadows moved beneath the blue waters. Swarms of creatures shimmered under the sea, but only in the dark places. In the light coral and seaweed were waiting to snag a swimmer and drag him down. The sailors spoke true, the sea here is dangerous, and when the darkness came, the beasts would surely set upon them. Turning back, he looked into the gash of the mountain. The darkness was all consuming as was the odor.

He unslung a satchel tied on his back and opened it. Removing a small metal lamp, he placed a wick inside. Taking a ball of hard wax shaped like a small amphora, he broke off the neck and poured oil into the lamp. Turning his back on the wind he struck up tinder and steel. In short order he had a burning wick. Shielding the flame from the wind he melted some wax and sealed the lamp oil container. Repositioning the satchel on his back, he lifted the lamp, and entered the darkness.

Deep within, the moaning sound of the cavern cried out to his ear. Periodically he stopped, shielded the lamplight, listened, then moved ahead. For the most part the path was level and void of rubble, but the stench grew in intensity. It was a smell he knew, the stink of decay.

Cocooned within the bubble of light he could only see a step forward and a step back. The moaning grew louder, and he became aware of other sounds too, the cries of men and women in desperate suffering.

Ahead he could see the dim glow of torchlight. He shielded the lamp and moved on, only to stumble over something slick and malleable. Lowering the lamp, he drew back in amazement. He was ankle deep in a pile of dismembered hands and feet, all in various stages of decay, the least on top. The pile peaked as high as his head, and the circumference was twenty cubits wide. He looked up. A hole in the roof showed the flicker of a torch fifty feet above. Was he too late? Had Bulvife already been maimed, or worse? He moved around the pile and toward the light ahead.

Cut into the stone a set of stairs went up. Putting down the lamp he listened for a moment, then moved up. The light became brighter. The cries of the suffering weighed on his ears as he topped the stairs, and a wide hall came into view. At one end a fire blazed. Next to it a bellows was connected and many metal instruments hung on wooden posts near a wide table. It looked like a blacksmiths shop, and the smell of burnt flesh hung in the air.

"No, please, I've done nothing..." a male voice cried out.

Benhargan shrank back into the shadows and moved to a pillar of stone. He looked out and watched the scene. A thin man with a beard was dragged to the table and strapped down. A stout fellow in a cowl and leather apron heated an iron in the fire. Cries and pleading were constant, then came the screaming. Agony was no stranger to Benhargan, he had heard it on the battlefield many times. Men called for their mothers, fathers, and gods as pain overwhelmed them. This was different. This sound made Benhargan angry, where the latter had roused no feelings whatsoever.

Meat was flayed from the man, and burns were applied. Finally, the man in the apron took a hatchet and in one stroke took off the foot of the man on the table. The screaming stopped. The wound was cauterized and wrapped in cloth. "Take him and release him into the city," the man in the apron said. He was removed from the room by two others, and the man in the apron walked over to a hole and tossed the severed limb into it.

BULVIFE LAMENTED, "THAT son of a dog. Leaving me here to rot, I curse the very name Benhargan." A trapdoor opened at the base of the wooden door, and he heard something slide in. Slowly he approached and bent down, the smell of burnt meat filled his nose. "About time," he said loudly.

"Shut up!" came a gruff voice from beyond. "You'll sing a different tune soon." Footsteps vanished.

In the darkness he ate the meat. It mattered little what it was, he'd never been too picky when it came to eating. Growing up in the harsh lands of Cimmeria, a boy learns to eat anything, or be eaten. He chuckled at the thought. When he'd finished, he set the plate down and pissed into it. "Enjoy you curs," he said. If he lived to be a thousand years old, he'd have his revenge on these men, and Benhargan.

He sat in the darkness for what seemed like many hours. All the while he pined for his moment of action. The clicking sound of someone removing the peg from the cell door alerted him. A soft orange glow appeared, first as a crack, then the light enveloped him. He shielded his eyes.

"Grab him!"

Five men rushed in. Bulvife moved like a snake, struck the first man in the throat, the second in the knee, but the third, fourth, and fifth took him to the ground. His hands were bound, all the while the moans of the injured men played delight in his ears.

"You'll pay for that!" A fat man with the torch said.

"You'd have better luck sucking Crom's hairy balls than making me pay for that," Bulvife laughed.

"You'll not be so arrogant in a moment. Bring him; it is your time," the fat man said.

They dragged Bulvife down a dirty hallway and out into a wide room. Torches on the walls illuminated some of it, but it was clear that the roof was high, hidden in the darkness. Ahead, a table, instruments, and fire came into view. They forced him onto the table, and looped ropes around his wrists. One of the men groaned in pain suddenly. Bulvife looked over to see the tip of a brass blade sticking out of the man's chest. The other one gasped then was beheaded. The man at his feet turned to run, but blood colored the air as his spine became exposed; he tumbled down a hole in the floor with a thud. A large man in a leather apron turned to him, took his sword and cut his bonds. Bulfive sprung from the table ready to fight.

Pulling the apron and cowl off, Benhargan narrowed his gaze at Bulvife, "You didn't think I was going to leave you here, did you?"

"I did," Bulvife said. "I was plotting your death; it is wise you returned to quell my ill temper."

A shout echoed down a passageway. "They found the torturer's body," Benhargan said as he turned and rushed toward the stairs. "This way."

Down the stairs they flew and into the passage. Benhargan grabbed his lamp that was sitting on the last step and led the way as they ran with great speed. He moved around the pile of limbs, over the body of the man from above, and rushed headlong through turns and twists until natural light showed. They emerged onto the ledge and Benhargan could see it was dusk. The creatures of the water were invisible in the low light and no ship's lights could be seen.

Bulvife stopped. "Now where?"

A shout was heard behind them and Benhargan turned to see torches in the darkness of the tunnel. He pointed over the ledge, "We'd better start down."

They reached the boat, and it took both men to free it and send it back into the waves. Bulvife pulled at the oars and the small boat broke through the tide and into the sea beyond. Arrows flew past them, one sticking into the boat at Benhargan's feet. There was not enough room for both men to row, so Bulvife stayed at his post pulling hard, recovering, dropping the oars into the water and pulling again.

"How did you know it was me coming out of the cell?" Bulvife said.

"The torturer complained that the next victim destine for the rack would fight like a wild cat, not passive like the others." Another arrow flew past them and landed in the water. "Who else could he be talking about but a Cimmerian."

Finally, they were out of range and hidden by the coming darkness. "Here, Cimmerian, we've waited," a sailor shouted from the darkness and tossed them a rope.

Benhargan seized it and pulled the boat to the ship. "Pull up your anchor and get underway. The Tarans will not sit over this insult." As he finished his sentence, in the distance a ship's bow lantern appeared near the cape.

"Did you get it?" Bulvife said as he stepped onto the deck.

"Yes, it took a few days, breaking some bones, and busting out some teeth, but I got it. Grimface the mystic will be pleased."

"He should have told us of these trials before we left him."

"I don't think he's a very good mystic," Benhargan laughed. The boat moved under sail. "Let us forget the bitter labors we've each had." He looked at one of the sailors, "Fetch a jar of beer. Now we drink." The man ran to the back of the boat.

"Here, I saved this for you," Bulvife said, cocked back his fist and struck Benhargan square in the jaw.

The man was immovable, smiled back, spit some blood and laughed. "I expected such, but, if you were angry why did you hit me like a little girl?"

Bulvife chuckled, "Because I knew it was the limit of what you could take."

They both drank and laughed as the ship sailed.

CHAPTER 2
THE REALM OF YI

EVEN FROM A DISTANCE the roar and flash from the dragon fire could be seen and heard. Bulvife came from the aft, "They're gaining on us, and they're armed with a flame machine."

"We might have to fight," Benhargan said.

Several sailors pulled on the ropes to loosen the sail and improve their speed. Each of them knew that if the Tarans captured their ship, it would be them in the cave of torture as well as their passengers. "But they have dragon fire. We will be roasted alive," one sailor cried.

"Your fear is contagious, stifle it," Bulvife chided. He turned to Benhargan and the Captain. "They have oars, and we have wind, and oars are winning. It is only a matter of time before we're in range of their ballista, arrows and fire."

Benhargan looked back at the sleek two-story galley cutting through the new dawn waters. Its long ram crested a wave then plunged down again. A group of sailors on the prow pulled down on a lever and fire shot fifty feet ahead of the ship. "They're determined. What if we turn and ram one side of their oars, sheering off half of them?"

The captain looked grave, "Stupid Cimmerian, they're a ship of war, don't you think they thought of that already. By the time we'd put out the fire, fended off their boarding party they'd have another set of oars in the water and the ship would overtake us."

Bulvife laughed, "I have it. They can't keep rowing if we shrink their ranks; without oarsmen, the oars will be useless."

"By Crom, that's using that empty gourd of yours," Benhargan stated. "But how?"

"Do you still have the tools that Sven'la'gal the thief gave you?" Bulvife raised his eyebrows.

Benhargan moved to a chest on the deck and threw it open, "I have them here," he said.

"Didn't he have some climbing claws he claimed could scale any surface?"

"He did." Benhargan removed what looked like two iron handles with five sharp hooks each. "Here they are." He handed them to Bulvife.

Taking the hand-claws he looked around the deck. "That ram's bladder, fetch it me," he said as he pointed. A sailor retrieved it. He poured out the contents, blew it up, and tied the end. "Okay, pray that I can fend off the sea beast long enough to kill the oars men on that boat." Bulvife went to the bow. Turning back, he added, "Circle around and pick me up. Watch that their ballista doesn't sink you." He went over the side with a noiseless splash and vanished under the waves.

The captain shouted, "You're going to be killed."

Benhargan grunted, "They can't hear your warning. The dogs on the pursuing ship have the wind in their ears."

"I was yelling at your friend," the captain said.

"Don't be a fool," Benhargan chided, "Bulvife has done stupider things and lived to tell of it. The only ones in danger of death are those who pursue us."

"What is he doing?"

"A trick we used to traverse the Thunder River some years ago. Many a Pict paid with their lives that day."

A sailor came from the aft, "I see the wineskin but not the man."

"That's the point," Benhargan said. He'd traveled with Bulvife for many years now, and felled may a foe with the man. At the battle of Ur, he and Bulvife killed a hundred Picts each, and their chief. So jealous was the commander of the Zingaran army that he tried to have them both murdered. *We were doing something right that day*, he thought. So, he knew enough about Bulvife to know that when the dice were foul, he could count on him to keep a dagger from his back. "He'll rid us of that rabble. Now", he looked up at the captain, "bring us about."

The hull of the ship was approaching. Bulvife could hear the beat of the ship's drum while he sucked the air from the bladder. An oar cut into the water near his head. He reached out with the claws and snagged the hull just above the waterline. The oars recovered and again smashed into the water. He angled the claws and began climbing. Creeping between the poles, and up to the deck railing, he glanced over the edge and saw a few men near a ballista talking. Their backs were to him. He slipped over the railing, onto the deck and behind a row of amphora that stunk of sulfur. Peeking around the corner he could see that his arrival was unnoticed. Slipping his knife from its sheath he crept around the observation stand to the hatchway leading down. The beat of the drum was growing louder as he came to a door. Lifting the latch, he peeked inside; forty men per deck were seated and drawing the oars, one man rushed up and down the rows with water and a ladle. Another man beat the drum as the rowers pulled and recovered and pulled again. *Perhaps I should have planned this out better*, he thought. *Now what? Surely, I can't just stroll in and stab all these men.* He heard someone coming.

At the top of the stairs a surprised and shirtless sailor went silent and rigid as Bulvife's knife retracted from his throat. The whoosh of the fire machine filled the air and the stench of the pitch and oil reeked. Bulvife smiled. By Crom, that's the answer. He skulked onto the deck hiding by the stack of amphora. The pitch stench was present, and he cut the wax from the top and looked inside. Dark black pitch shifted with the roll of the ship. Toward the prow ten men stood manning the fire device. At one end was an open container, to the side was a plunger, and extending forward was a long tube with a flame at the end. The lever was raised, and five men made ready to pull down on the long handle.

"Fire," shouted a sailor wearing a feathered helmet.

Bulvife leapt onto the deck, an amphora raised above his head. With intense ferocity he threw the container at the men as they pulled down on the lever. The jar of sticky liquid struck the apparatus, covering the sailors as the flame shot forward, then the whole front of the ship burst into flame. The five men at the bow were immolated without a scream. The other five leapt from the ship. Two sailors rushed from the hold and fell to Bulvife's knife. Two more came and he chased them overboard as the bright orange flames raced back toward the aft. Three men abandoned the steering rudder and plunged overboard. He dashed to the railing. The ship bobbed up and down as sailors fled the hold and leapt into the water. He stood up on the rail, crouched and dove into the sea. He swam for a few minutes then turned to see the ship fully engulfed.

He swam for what seemed like an hour. From behind him a voice rang out, "Here, you stinking jackal," Benhargan shouted as he threw a rope to Bulvife. Clinging to the cord he was pulled up onto deck. "Ye stink of fish," Benhargan stated.

"Just like yer mother I'm sure," Bulvife responded.

Benhargan smiled and nodded, "I thought you were going to kill the oarsmen?"

"Why kill one man at a time when fire can do many?" Bulvife said.

"No matter, the oars are stopped, and how you did it is for Crom alone to understand." Benhargan broke the top on a jar of beer, took a drink and handed it to Bulvife. "Now we're free to see the magician."

The crew cheered and the sail was tightened. The ship came about and headed for safe harbor up the coast.

Night came and the sea darkened. They took shelter in a cove near the Barachen Islands. With deliberate intent Benhargan broke the neck of a wine jar and drank heartily. Bulvife looked out at the jungle as a roar echoed out to the ship.

"What do you see that makes you worried?" Benhargan said.

Bulvife turned and sat down, took a wine jar and tore off the wax top. He drank for a moment then shrugged, "I can see beasts in the forest, unnatural things large and manlike. They lurk from the jungle, approach the water then retreat."

Benhargan shuddered and took another drink, "Beasts that Grimface warned us about?"

"I can only guess." Bulvife drank and wiped his mouth.

"He said that the beasts roam the forest looking for man-flesh to eat."

Bulvife stood up and looked out at the island again, "Look," he pointed into the jungle. A faint pinkish glint could be seen through the mangrove. It hovered there for a moment then vanished into the dark. "What by Crom was that?"

"You tell me, I didn't see anything."

A sailor came by. "What is it you see?"

"Something pink, a glow like from a large gem."

The man looked thoughtful, "It is the Yi. It is said to inhabit the island, keeping vigil for trespassers. The legend says it has one large gem for an eye and can see all."

"A gem you say?" Benhargan stood up.

"A gem the size of your head, or bigger," the sailor added.

"But no man has set foot upon the island and lived to tell of its treasures," the Captain said as he came from under the awning at the aft. "Many fools have ventured there, their boats litter the beaches. None have returned."

"Prepare the boat, I want to see this Yi firsthand," Benhargan said.

"You'd better put in some jars of wine too," Bulvife added as he moved toward the rowboat.

The two Cimmerians cast off the small boat and Benhargan took up the oars. Bulvife prepared their bows and sat back with his sword across his lap. "A gem the size of your head, that's a big gem."

Benhargan grunted, "Be glad it's not the size of my member, or we'd never be able to carry it back in the boat!"

Bulvife chuckled, "Ya, if we dropped it, it could be lost in one of the cracks in the boat."

They both laughed then grew somber. "I have a strange feeling," Bulvife said.

"Good or bad?"

"If it was good, I wouldn't have mentioned it."

Benhargan looked over his shoulder at the shore, "Don't worry."

Bulvife looked dubiously at the man. An earth-shattering roar echoed from the jungle. "If it be our day to die, so be it. Crom will know our hearts, and that we died for love of battle."

"If it be now, I'll have a go at Crom's concubines, then he'll know I've arrived. Now, let's see what lurks on this island."

The boat slid up onto the sandy beach. The two men climbed out. The sounds of the jungle were unnerving. A black silhouette of the ship could be seen in the cove bobbing up and down. Benhargan secured his sword belt and took up his bow and quiver. Bulvife followed as they slipped into the dense and dark foliage of the forest. Neither man was an amateur at tracking and stealth. They were rangers, skilled at hunting, both man and beast. They moved silently through the underbrush and vines. The darkness was powerful, but their eyes were accustomed to such.

In the trees things lurked. Massive hairy creatures moved from branch to branch, their glowing eyes watching the two men. Benhargan stopped while Bulvife notched an arrow. Benhargan made a sign with his hands, something ahead, a building perhaps. He parted a broad leafy plant and stepped into a temple court. Massive flagstones were laid out a hundred to one side and a hundred long. They were five cubits wide if a hand and set with such precision that no jungle life poked up between the seams. The temple lay in darkness, shattered, broken upon the wheel of time. A roar echoed and all the noise in the jungle fell silent.

"It's getting closer," Benhargan stated.

"The creature that's been tracking us?"

"Yes," Benhargan said.

Bulvife moved to a row of broken and black columns. Twenty of the cylinders lay prone, felled from their bases, and twenty remained standing, an homage to ancients who wrought them. A powerful smell fell over him and he swooned with sudden delight and passion. "Black lotus," he said as Benhargan skulked up.

"Yes, the scent is heavy, and pleasing," Benhargan stated. He moved toward a raised platform and more columns. He froze. Something behind them shook a grove of trees. Notching an arrow, he formed himself against one of the columns. Bulvife came along side and did likewise. "Look behind us," Benhargan commented.

Bulvife turned just as a man came at them with a flint knife. He let loose an arrow and the man fell clutching the shaft that protruded from his chest. Three more came, weapons of obsidian ready for the kill. He loosed his sword and intercepted them.

Benhargan waited as a creature emerged from the dark jungle. It was as large as two elephants, and covered in fur that glowed a pinkish hue. A horn as long as a man's arm extended from its muzzle, and it fixed its gaze on him. It roared and the stones shook.

One of the natives stopped, turned, and ran back into the ruins of the temple. The other two fell to Bulvife's sword. He turned to see the beast charging.

"It comes," Benhargan said and launched three arrows in succession.

"Flee you fool," Bulvife shouted and pulled at his friend. They ran further into the temple. Behind them they could hear the creature slam into the columns and roar into the hall after them. Into the darkness they ran, only realizing that there was no sky above, and no monster in pursuit. Bulvife stopped. They were in utter darkness. "What now?"

Benhargan spoke, "How should I know, you led the way like a scared rabbit."

Bulvife chuckled, "Not scared, tactful," he said. He knelt, took tinder from his pouch and struck flint to steel. A small yellow flame followed and the room lit up like a chief's treasure box. Gold was piled high in the corners, plates of brass reflected the light, gems of many colors were embedded in the walls and littered the floor, and the light made the room spin with color. Benhargan scooped up a handful of yellow, red, and blue gems and tucked them into his shirt. Bulvife took gold chains, brass bars, and silver coins.

"There," Bulvife pointed into a large pile of gold coins. Something large was there, and pink. They dug into the pile then the light began to fade. Benhargan rushed back to the fire and put some slivers of wood on it and rushed back. They dug and dug until the massive gem was revealed. The light dominated the other gems, and it took the two men to pull it free from the gold and lay it on the ground. A howl erupted and darkly skinned men rushed at them from several doorways. Each native fell dead before they could land a blow. More sounds from outside, could be heard, many men, like a tribe gathering.

"Grab what you can...wait," Benhargan knelt down; the ground under the stones and metals was dark. "Quickly," he said as he slapped the dark dirt onto his arms. The light from their fire faded and the two men rubbed the dark soil on themselves. "Now help me fill this chest with gems and gold."

KULAKI CALLED INTO the god's den. His men had gone in there to ferret out the interlopers and vanished. He hoped that the gods had not come awake, not like the cetremer had. The creature was a curse to his land and a ravenous beast that consumed flesh in mass. Just ahead in the darkness he saw two of his men come into the moonlight. They carried a third. He called to them, but they seemed not to hear. The man they carried looked dead, for he could see the blackness of blood all over his skin. He shouted again, and they vanished into the ruins and jungle. He turned to his son, "They must be going back to camp. Run ahead and see that our brother is prepared for his travel to the gods." The boy sped off into the darkness.

"Kulaki," called a voice from within the den. One of the men he had sent crawled forth. "They still live…" He collapsed.

Kulaki looked at his warriors. "They have deceived us. Track them!" He lifted his club and they rushed into the forest with murder upon their lips.

CHAPTER 3
GRIMFACE'S FOLLY

THE BODY WAS HEAVY. Bulvife held the legs at the knees and Benhargan the arms at the pits. In the distance a roar rattled the treetops. Some birds took flight and the hairy creatures that swung from the branches became still and silent. The heavy musky scent of the jungle filled Benhargan's nose, and he huffed as they carried the native over vines, past thick trunks, and around tangled bushes. In the silence the tramping of underbrush could be heard.

"They're onto us," Bulvife said between gulps of air.

"Just keep running."

"I could run faster if this body didn't weigh so much."

"We're fine, just keep moving."

They crashed through some dense underbrush and onto the beach. Ahead was the boat and they picked up speed. A few steps from the water Benhargan stopped and looked at the rotted conveyances. Boats littered the beach, some half buried in the sand, and others rotted mostly apart. "Up the beach," he said. The natives burst onto the beach, looked around then howled with rage. The pursuit was on again.

Rushing up and over a large black boulder, he and Bulvife leapt down into black sands. Ahead he could see a lone rowboat on the beach. "There it is, hurry."

The natives poured over the boulder and spilled onto the beach. Spears and arrows flew past the harried men as they threw the body into the boat. Bulvife shoved the craft from the shore and Benhargan pulled at the oars. The screams of the savages were suddenly eclipsed by the roar of the monster as it breached the forest and plunged onto the beach. The natives turned, half rushed towards the rocks, the others fled into the waters. Several were caught in mid run and torn apart. Benhargan watched as the beast devoured the remains, cocked back its head and let out a triumphant bellow.

Bulvife shrugged and put his sword back into its scabbard then wiped the sweat from his face. "The beast must have been tracking us all."

"No, just the savages. They were in such a rush to kill us that they forgot to move silent and surefooted," Benhargan stated.

The boat bumped against the side of the ship. Two sailors looked down. "What is it that you have?" one said.

"It's a savage," the other stated.

"Get a rope. Take the body onboard," Bulvife commanded.

"Don't drop it into the sea," Benhargan threatened, "or ye'll go in after it."

The two sailors knew the barbarians didn't make idle threats. Both disappeared and returned with rope. They dropped it over the side and the Cimmerian's secured the body. "Haul it up," Bulvife said. Both men climbed up and Benhargan tied the boat to the railing.

"He looks so little but is so heavy," one sailor said.

Landing heavy onto the deck a cascade of bloody gold and gems fell across the planks spilling out of the body. Bouncing out last came a massive pink gem that rolled to a halt against a barrel of water. The sailor's gasped. Bulvife could see the white part of their eyes as they stood over the loot.

"He was stuffed with treasure," one said.

"He was stuffed with our treasure," Benhargan stated with a stern look. The two sailors stepped back.

"We saw your escape," the captain commented coming from the aft. The Yi seemed a lustful beast hungering for your hides."

"If I had more time I'd make its head a dwelling for my new treasure," Benhargan said.

"And I would make its skin a tent for my harem," Bulvife stated.

Benhargan plunged his hand into the open body cavity of the native. He rifled around and produced a gold chain. "Stuck in the blood," he declared as he ran his hand around again and then nodded to Bulvife. The two men lifted the body and dumped it overboard. "Your usefulness is at an end," he said as the body splashed into the sea and sank into darkness.

"That's much wealth you've stolen," the captain eyed the bucket greedily.

Both Benhargan and Bulvife scooped up the gold and gems and put them into a bucket then plopped the giant gem on top, sealing the bucket. "The first man who touches that bucket will end up like the savage," Bulvife declared.

The captain smiled turned and walked back to his awning. "Sleep well barbarians, for tomorrow we will be along the Hyborian coast and near Argos. You can put ashore there."

Benhargan took the first watch. Two hours of sitting with his sword across his lap watching the sailors sleep made him crave battle and women. At times a sailor would stray from his bed and relieve himself over the side then return to his hammock or lump of cloth. The beast on shore often came onto the beach and looked out at the ship. Benhargan watched as the creature rolled around where it had made its kill, then lurk back into the jungle. As false dawn came Bulvife took over, but Benhargan slept light. By first light, the sailors prepared the ship for sail, and they got underway.

Hours passed as the sun came up over the blue waters. The Barachen islands fell far behind them and from time to time the spritely sea creatures raced alongside the ship. "Land ahead," shouted a sailor at the bowsprit. A sliver of land was visible, and it grew as the ship got closer. Benhargan watched the sea beasts break away and the gulls become plentiful. Several merchant ships appeared with colorful sails. The captain angled the ship toward a crescent shaped cove and dropped anchor. "Our bargain is fulfilled barbarian. Here is where we part company." Several sailors came, swords in hand.

"What is this?" demanded Benhargan.

"You can leave, but the bucket remains," the captain said.

Bulvife lifted back his head and belted out a tremendous laugh. "And you think you can keep our treasure with the force of these men?"

The sailors looked unsettled as their swords quaked in their hands. Benhargan's face betrayed no emotion. "You have been a fair Captain," he began, "but, who among your sailors, who have tasted the captain's lash would like to be Captain?" Men in the rabble looked at each other. "I'll give you half the gold in this bucket if you kill -."

"Perhaps we've been hasty," the captain began, "in demanding what is yours. If you were as gracious as a king, perhaps you'd leave us something extra for staying by your side on this adventure?"

Benhargan moved quickly and the captain clutched a bleeding throat. Blood pumped between his fingers and his eyes were wide with surprise. "I say again, who among you will be Captain now?"

A medium size swarthy fellow stepped from the ranks. "I Aziz will command this ship...if it pleases you?" The captain fell to his knees and onto his side as the deck grew crimson.

Again, Bulvife laughed, "It's of no concern to us who takes this ship. But remember what you've seen here and don't let your greed cause your blood to color the decks. He retrieved the ancient jar and waited for Benhargan to climb down into the rowboat. Handing the man, the bucket and jar, he descended. Pushing off the hull the rowboat began moving towards shore.

They watched as the ship grew smaller. The sailors took up the anchor and set the sail, and the ship moved away as a body was dumped over the side. "I was about to give that fool a hand full of gems," Benhargan said.

Bulvife looked surprised, "Really, a jackal like that?"

"He did keep the ship at the cliff when we escaped the Taran cave."

"He's now with his god and probably complaining bitterly," Bulvife chuckled. "Should have known not to try your patience."

"Of little mind it is," Benhargan said, "Let' s set our sights on finding the magician." He pulled at the oars.

Bulvife picked some dried blood from the giant gem. "He said he'd be at the Green Jade tavern."

"Yes, and he owes us much. He'd better remove this curse that colors our mind and dulls our wits." He angled the boat and it glided onto the stony beach. They both climbed out; Bulvife carried the bucket, and Benhargan the jar.

"This bucket contains enough wealth that we can both live like kings," Bulvife commented.

Benhargan looked bemused. "A king buys a few valuable haram girls or concubines to enjoy, a couple jars of sweet mead and a bull for a feast, then the bucket is empty. We can buy many a cheap whore, drink new beer and wine until our eyes bleed, and feast in the taverns like gods until we shrivel with age," he stated. They began walking. "How far to the city?"

"Maybe seven leagues. You know we'll smell it long before we see it," Bulvife added as he led the way along a path into a stand of trees. The wind blew steadily as he picked his way through the thorny thickets and twisted briars. After an hour they stumbled out onto a dirt path. "This way," he declared.

The trail led to a dirt road, and that road led to a cobblestone highway. Darkness began to fall. "A strange light ahead," Benhargan stated. He could see a torch against a stone wall that expelled a green mist. He was cautious as he realized it was not just a wall, but a large building at the side of the road. A faint and eerie green glow seemed to emit from the whole structure. "If ever your ranger skills were sharp, keep an extra vigil with this place," he said to Bulvife as a shiver ran up his spine.

"Perhaps we should give it quarter and move to the south," Bulvife stated as he continued to move toward it.

"I can't seem to stop myself from approaching," Benhargan said.

A shimmering white ghostly presence appeared at the road. A beautiful woman in a flowing white toga turned to them and beckoned them hither. The jar in Benhargan's arms started to glow, and he could feel subtle warmth emit from it as they got closer.

"I can't stop," Bulvife said.

"Nor I." Benhargan added. The jar became hot, and he dropped it. It shattered on the ground and a glowing hunk of metal fell out. They both stopped moving.

The spirit transformed and standing before them was a terrible sight. The creature stood twice the height of a man and was covered in black scales. A single horn protruded from its forehead, and its glowing red eyes burnt both men as it leveled its gaze on them.

"I'd wager the creature can't leave that place," Bulvife stated. "Or, it would have devoured us already."

Benhargan tried reaching for his sword, yet it was too hot to touch. "This demon has fouled us," he shouted.

"It wants the metal fragment that Grimface desired. It must be powerful magic." Bulvife concentrated on his legs and took a step backward. "Focus," he said, "think of moving your legs backward." In a few moments the two men were walking backwards, away from the monster.

The green structure wavered and faded revealing a ruinous wall and some pillars of stone. A man wearing a green robe with yellow edges stepped out, looked at the barbarians with eyes as wide as plates, then ran down the road toward the city. Bulvife notched an arrow and let fly. The man fell with a yelp and clutched the arrow in his thigh. Benhargan picked up the piece of metal that had fallen from the jar, removed his sword and approached the man. "Who sent you, and why do you want this hunk of metal," he asked.

The man rolled on his side. "You Cimmerians disgust me, you're ignorant and brutes!"

Bulvife approached and removed his knife from its sheath, "We'll know the answers soon enough."

The city of Kurs stood out in the wilderness like a boil on the nose of a whore. All around the walls were huts, and two story structures made half of stone and the other half timber and mud. Smoke saturated the air and the first buildings Benhargan and Bulvife came across were the tannery and the dyer. The stench from both was nearly overwhelming. Beyond the reeking dye pits and tanner pools, they came to a miller's hut and next the herbalists. Finally, they saw private abodes of those who called the city protector.

At the tall wooden palisades Bulvife stopped and called up to a guard, "You, let two travelers in."

The guard looked down, spit once then called to someone beyond the wall. The gate slowly opened. Once inside the two men headed for a triangular set of buildings built of mudbrick and wooden beams. A wooden shingle hung out front and showed a jar of beer and a leg of fowl. They entered.

Darkness filled the room even though there were candles along each wall and braziers on the floor. Long wooden tables were set up in the middle with benches to accommodate the dozens of men inside. Women mingled, and horns of beer and wine were hoisted and drank. The smell of sweat, and stale spirits vied for attention among the cooking meats and stews. On one table meat, bread, and roots were placed, and men sitting there feasted with abandon. A narrow set of stairs went up to a second level where the moaning of pleasure could be heard.

"There he is," stated Benhargan.

The two men made their way toward a dark-skinned man of equal stature to themselves. He looked up and acknowledged them, then stood and walked up the stairs. They followed. Once at the top the man motioned for them to enter a room and they stood facing each other.

"Did you bring it?"

"We have it here," Benhargan said pulling the metal from his belt and handing it over.

The man smiled under his dark mustache, "Yes, this is it."

"Now, what of the curse of Ottin'bar?" Bulvife said. "We've done your bidding Grimface, now you must do what you promised."

Grimface observed the bucket, "I see you found something tasty."

"Our compensation for the trip," Benhargan stated.

"Perhaps..." Grimface sat on a rope bed and examined the metal piece. "The curse has made you weak both of mind and body. You think it affects your soul too?" He put the metal into a leather pouch. "I need your help to do something else."

Bulvife laughed, "Is it not enough that we've retained this for you?"

"It is not." Grimface looked up at the two Cimmerians, "There is one last piece I need, but I cannot get it myself. I need you two to accompany me, and deal death to the guards of my foe."

"For a price," Benhargan said.

"You are in no position to demand. The curse will remain upon your head until these items are gathered, and Ottin'bar is defeated."

"It will be of little concern to me after I gut you," Benhargan's face made clear his serious nature.

Grimface laughed, "Death?" He stood up. "What you two know about death couldn't even fill a cupped hand. No matter, I can help the pain and weakness you feel from the curse to be absent for a time." He waved his hand, chanted some un-worldly words. He shook violently, then fell back. "There, now I must sleep for two days. It is not easy to block another's curse," he labored. "You will guard me as I sleep, and when I awake, we will discuss your compensation for your further services." The normal appearance of his eyes changed to terrifying demon eyes as he fell into a deep sleep.

"Do you think we should have told him of the demon?" Bulvife stated.

Benhargan sat down with his back to the outside wall. "Why worry a troubled mind such as his."

"Now what," Bulvife asked.

"We wait. You guard first. Wake me in two hours."

"Just enough time for me to enjoy a woman," Bulvife stated with a grin, "and a jar of wine."

Benhargan chuckled, "I said two hours, not two minutes."

"Sleep and pray I don't cut your throat for lack of entertainment."

"I'll sleep like a deer in the forest knowing all the tigers are at rest," Benhargan said putting his sword across his lap and closing his eyes.

Bulvife laughed, "Sleep well my friend, if you die in your sleep, tell Crom he is a son-of-a-bitch."

"He knows," Benhargan said then closed his eyes and fell into a light sleep.

CHAPTER 4
THE TREK TO BABATEH

THE SOUNDS OF MERRIMENT in the tavern below raged nonstop all night. By first light the patrons were passed out, murdered, or left for greener pastures. Benhargan strayed from the room and descended the stairs. A half-eaten leg of mutton was on the floor near the last step, and he picked it up. He fetched a pitcher of wine and ascended the stairs again. Bulvife was asleep in the corner of the room. Grimface was on the bed. Down the hall a woman made a rude remark and shoved a man from her chamber, "Come back when you have more brass to spend," she said then vanished back into her room.

The pains in Benhargan's joints were constant now, even with the help of Grimface's magic. He ignored it as best as possible, but he needed a good dose of wine to quell it. It was not long ago that he and his friend robbed the tomb of Hotep et Epen. Ottin'bar paid them well and they should have known better, but the money was too good, and between the wine, women, and black lotus, they swore an oath that they would do his bidding. The curse fell upon their heads when they broke the sacred seal that bound the ancient relic. It seemed insignificant; the relic was a stick tipped with a dial studded with crystals. When they presented Ottin'bar with the item, he drugged them with poisoned wine, and left them unpaid and cursed. The deceiver fled, and it was only blind luck, or will of the gods that the two Cimmerians came across Grimface the magician. Over wine they commiserated about Ottin'bar, and the three men realized they had a common enemy.

Bulvife snorted and came awake. He sat up and rubbed his eyes, "Why do you stare like a goat at a sacrifice?"

Benhargan looked down and handed his friend the pitcher. "Just thinking on how to kill Ottin'bar." He took a bite of the mutton.

"I feel the pain too now," Bulvife stood and went to a bucket in the corner of the room and relieved himself. "The magician told us he needs the other parts of that amulet to destroy that fatherless whore. And it makes sense why Ottin's agent wanted to steal the metal from us."

"He failed and now Ottin'bar will become more desperate." Benhargan spun around, the tip of his brass sword pressed softly against a woman's neck. He took another bite of the mutton. She looked at the men with eyes full of fear. "You nearly lost your life for foolishness," he told her.

She swallowed hard and stepped back, "I have a message for your master from the temple of Baal."

Benhargan regarded her with a lustful eye, "Baal, eh? I hear that the priestesses of Baal make for fine riding in that house." He shoved the mutton into Bulvife's arms.

"I am not permitted to entertain lovers. I am betrothed to Baal only." She looked at Bulvife who also looked at her feminine attributes with unabashed lust. "I must whisper a message into your master's ear," she pointed at Grimface.

Benhargan lunged and gripped the girl's dress, tearing away her brown shift and throwing himself upon her. She cried out.

Bulvife knocked Benhargan to the side, "I'll go first," he lustily lamented and prepared to mount her.

Benhargan clubbed Bulvife, Bulvife struck Benhargan with the mutton joint, and a fight erupted. They crashed from one side of the room to the other then fell across Grimface. The magician sat up, his demon eyes erupting like fire as he shouted, "Be still!" He stood and with some invisible force pushed Bulvife and Benhargan to the opposite side of the room and held them against the wall. His eyes fell on the girl, and he gasped, "You fools, it's Ottin'bar." The girl changed shape before their eyes. Ottin'bar stood in the doorway.

Shock settled over Benhargan, for he quite nearly mounted the man.

"He is using a spell you idiot," Grimface shouted. Ottin'bar looked enraged and with one hand grabbed the barbarian's treasure bucket and with the other threw a gray powder into the air as he dashed from the room. "Don't breathe." Grimface grabbed the urine bucket and splashed it over the blanket on the bed. "Cover your mouths and keep the blanket over you as we leave," He covered himself, Bulvife, and Benhargan. They moved from the room, into the hall, and down the stairs. At the bottom he pulled the blanket off and threw it into the fire pit. Turning to a haggard old man who watched them he spoke, "Seal up the second room on the second level. None will live after being in that chamber now." Looking at Bulvife and Benhargan with contempt his eyes changed to normal, and he narrowed his gaze. "You two, what a pretty bit of guarding you've accomplished. You let our enemy walk into our camp, and my sleep be disturbed. Now, we must quickly get to the river and wash, for if there is any of that dust on us, it will kill us soon."

"Why did you cover the blanket with piss?" Bulvife said.

Benhargan looked angry, "Forget the stinking blanket, what about our treasure?"

"Ottin'bar has your treasure now, and the urine blocks the dust from activating." Grimface led the way out the door. "If you wish to live and one day extract your revenge, follow me."

Bulvife dunked under the cold and clear river water. Popping up he shook his short dark hair, "He will have to suffer a thousand deaths to satisfy me."

Benhargan stood on the bank, "He will bleed for such an offense."

"Ottin'bar is no fool, and if it wasn't for your uncontrolled urges, he surely would have spoken the magic into my sleeping ear. I would now be a shambling slave of his to command, and you two would be stripped of your flesh for his amusement."

"We should tell you that we were attacked six days ago on the road to Kurs. A man in a yellow robe summoned a demon to try and steal the fragment," Bulvife stated.

"The robe was not yellow, it was green with yellow on the edges, and there was a green building in a fog," Benhargan said.

Grimface put his hand to his chin and sat on a rock. "It must be his servant Mul'ah Toc. He is known for the demon arts. The building was in the underworld as was the demon, like looking into these clear waters and seeing a fish. It is no wonder Ottin'bar found us in Kurs."

Bulvife swam out into the gentle current then back. "We had to cut his nose off, and when we told him his ears were next, he told us Ottin'bar wished the metal fragment to be his."

Grimface reclined. "What of the demon?"

"It vanished and did us little harm," Benhargan stated.

Grimface nodded, "Of course it did, or you two would not still be here. What became of Mul'ah?"

"I cut his throat and left him to bleed in the road," Benhargan stated then dunked under the water.

"But you did not kill him," Grimface said.

"He is dead," Benhargan commented.

"He is not dead," Grimface shook his head.

Benhargan stood, "What?"

"You failed to kill him. Though you bled him, and maybe ruined his voice, he is still walking and doing Ottin's bidding."

"How do you know this?" Benhargan demanded.

"Because he is there with twenty men," Grimface pointed across the river. The nose-less creature was plain to see atop a brown steed. Among his ranks were men in armor with lance and sword.

"It is a pretty smile you have now below your chin," Bulvife called out. Mul'ah became visibly agitated and touched the scar along his neck. He spoke not, but moved his hands and the twenty men fanned out to either side and began crossing the river.

"Since your master took our treasure, we will have to exact the account from your bones," Benhargan said as he removed his sword from its scabbard.

"And twenty-one men will rot in the sun beside this river today," Bulvife stated as he reached his bow, took three arrows in hand and notched one.

Mul'ah backed his horse up a few paces. It was clear that the mage struggled to speak. Grimface stood on the bank. "He cannot utter his evil magic," he said. "But my voice still floats a note." He let go with a burst of song and the waters began to vibrate. Several of the opposing horses panicked and threw their riders into the deep water. The men vanished from sight and were swept down river. The others continued to come. From down the river something formed taking shape into a human like visage. It came toward the horsemen. The upstream aggressors stopped to look. The thing came close; it had no legs only a white mist connecting it to the water. The face was like green algae, and its hands were bony like claws. The eyes were vacant, but its mouth bore needle like fangs. All the while Grimface sang.

Benhargan charged the transfixed men upstream, felling one man's horse and sending him into the clear waters. Bulvife let fly three arrows in succession, each finding home in the neck or chest of a rider. The water-creature reached the downstream horsemen. A screeching carried over Grimface's song. Biting and ripping, it leapt upon each horseman with vicious wrath. Horses screamed, men tried to defend, and the waters colored red. The monster tore all the living things in its path to bloody shreds.

Upstream, the remaining horsemen panicked and tried to get back across the river. Mul'ah sat in the same place, frustration written upon his face as his hands moved and his lips opened and closed but no words emerged. Benhargan grabbed the reins of a horse, pulled the rider down and boarded the beast. He charged across the river in pursuit of the fleeing men, then spun around, and as he passed Mul'ah, took the man's head in one pass. Grimface silenced and the monster vanished. The bodies floated silently down the river and past the rapids. Bulvife grabbed up three more arrows and turned back to see the battle evaporate.

"What was that thing?" Bulvife said.

"If you were a bit smarter you might have been frightened by it," Grimface laughed. "It was a water spirit, a dracquel. If disturbed it can kill man and beast if they stray too close to the water."

On the other side of the river Benhargan dismounted and kicked Mul'ah's head into the river. "Drink with your friends' you fiend!" The head bounced against a rock and Benhargan thought he could see the eyes blink as it vanished below the water.

"Quickly, we must get to the walled city of Babateh. It is there that we will get the last piece of the puzzle and sow the seeds of Ottin'bar's demise!"

"And what of our treasure?" Benhargan demanded.

"He has it, and much more," Grimface stated. "More treasures than you can comprehend," he laughed. "The city is upriver and to the north. Let us go now."

Grimface stopped at a crossroads. Looking back, he could see the two barbarians, like animals eyeing the surrounding countryside looking for hints of danger. "Is the pain growing?"

Bulvife grunted, "No more pain than the weight of a moth on the edge of a knife."

"And you barbarian?" Grimface looked at Benhargan.

"Like eating the porridge, they serve at the Gray Lion," he winked at Bulvife, and both men chuckled.

"And don't forget the pissing sickness. It is much less painful than that," Bulvife stated.

Grimface shook his head, "Fools, I am saddled with fools."

"No more the fools than a man who surrounds himself with fools for a plot of revenge that can only lead to their deaths," Bulvife added.

Grimface laughed too, "Maybe so. How far do you think we have to Babateh?"

"Ten leagues if we quicken our pace," Bulvife said.

"We could shorten it to five leagues if we carry Grimface," Benhargan said.

Grimface turned and began walking north. "You'll not carry me. If I desire it, I would fly."

The laughter slowed, then stopped, and the two Cimmerians followed as Grimface strolled with little care. They walked several leagues. High white clouds dotted the sky. In the distance the green and tan of the grass waved over rolling hills. They crossed the river many times until the road headed away from the snaking water. Slowly the terrain rose up hills and fell into valleys, and ahead of them were a set of mountains, red, brown, and gray. Trees began to appear as if taking over the vigil of the rolling grasslands. Oak and birch became numerous, as did the underbrush, and brambles. The unpaved and rutted road cut like a knife through the trees and briars and wound like the lace of a bracer through the wildlands. By the time they passed under the natural stone arch of Keelfort, six leagues had passed, and night was growing in the east.

"These gates are dangerous," Bulvife said.

Grimface knew of the bandits in the high mountains. "We can shelter in caves not far from here. Not many know of them, and those that do are a'feared to go near them."

"Feared of what?" Benhargan said.

"Ghosts," Grimface stated sardonically.

"Then let us go sleep with ghosts this night," Benhargan blustered as he took the lead.

The jagged opening looked like the teeth of a monster. As Benhargan looked on, he could reasonably be sure that the shape of the hillside was skull like. He watched as Grimface went into the cavern and came out with a gray sheet which he secured to a pole and anchored the four corners with twine. Under it he placed a candle on a rock and lit it. The sheet came alive in an eerie gray-white glow.

"What are you doing," Benhargan said.

"The ghost of Sul pass," Grimface laughed. "Bandits will not dare approach with our ghost on watch."

Bulvife came out from the cave. "I'm done stacking those dark stones as you asked."

"Good, now go in and make a fire in the pit." Grimface turned and entered the cave. "None will disturb us this night with the ghost out front and his army of ghosts in the cave."

As the fire rose in the pit, the dark stones emitted a ghastly light. Large blocks of a green crystal amplified the firelight and bathed them all in its emerald color. Grimface lay on a flat stone and fell fast asleep.

"Come," said Benhargan to Bulvife. They exited the cave and walked to the narrow pass. "Look you and remember," he turned and pointed at Grimface's handy work.

"It would scare most mortal men," Bulvife said. "Chills my blood seeing the ghost in front and the green light coming from the cave."

Benhargan grunted, "Magicians know how to deceive well. I wonder what deception we suffer at his hand?"

"He is cunning indeed," stated Bulvife. "Let us take our rest among the ghosts now." They returned to the cave. Again, Benhargan and Bulvife took turns watching the entrance. By dawn, they were ready to move again.

They passed through the last mountain gate and a wide valley appeared. At one end was a high mountain looking blood red in the morning light. At the other end a dark lake that looked like black glass. The valley filled with trees and wild grasses was inviting, and they entered without challenge. Far to the north they could see the ocher colored walls of Babateh. Even in the dull light of the morning they could see the white smoke of a thousand fires burning within the city.

"Have you ever been to Babateh," Grimface asked.

"Never," Benhargan stated.

"When I came from Cimmeria I stayed in this valley," Bulvife added. "A herdsman tried to rape me, and I broke his skull."

Grimface spoke over his shoulder, "None in the city will care of that. They only care for what happens in the city. Beware of the city laws here. The king who made them sees that they are enforced."

"More so than Tara?" Bulvife said.

"More so than those in Taraturn," stated Grimface. "We will enter through the sewer. I know someone who will shelter us, but we must not be seen entering, or Ottin'bar will know his days are short."

"All I want is to wear Ottin'bar's skin, and make him look upon it," Benhargan said.

"He will have a hard time seeing it if we cut out his eyes first," Bulvife brandished his hunting knife.

"Then, we will just have to wait to blind him. I wonder if some salt may be had, it will do wonders for his last moments."

"Be still," Grimface chided. "Do you think he will stand for such? He is a powerful magician and will be only vulnerable when we have the last fragment. Until then, your arrows and swords will be put to better use on the guards of the witch whom we will visit, for she holds the last of the amulet."

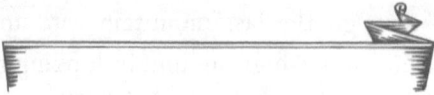

CHAPTER 5
THE WITCH, THE CARRION AND THE DUEL

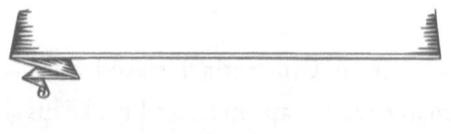

IF A MAN STOOD IN THE middle of the street, he could not extend his arms fully to either side without touching the walls of the adjacent building. The warren of streets led upward, and Grimface seemed to know where he was going. Benhargan and Bulvife followed closely for they both knew that if they became separated, they might not leave the city alive. In the distance a child could be heard squalling, dogs barked, and women yelled at lovers and husbands. Drunks mumbled in the dark alcoves and doorways and every now and again the caterwaul of a cat echoed in the streets.

"Your friend did not seem very hospitable," Benhargan said to Grimface.

"He knows the penalty for harboring we three." Grimface dodged to the side narrowly missing the dumping of human waste from a third story window. The filth spattered across the road and bathed the walls in a murky gray. "By tomorrow's dawn we will have slipped out and Babateh will be just a memory for us."

They maneuvered up the shadowed streets until Grimface stopped at an arched doorway. Benhargan came alongside, "Green fields? Fountains? On top of this mountain?" he said surprised.

"This mountain has springs that bubble up and was once a sacred hilltop. It is said that the god Hun made the goddess Elva from a piece of his own rib here, then both forged man and woman from the red clay of the pools and filled them with the breath of life."

A drunk stumbled toward them, eyed the three men, then turned and slumped into a doorway. The door opened and he was dragged inside the darkness.

"The witch lives on the other side of these green fields. She is a woman of some prominence and keeps her faith with Elva the Goddess."

"It matters not to me who she prays to. We will doom the guards and you have a free hand," Bulvife said.

"We will wait till dark then we can slip into her compound." Grimface knelt down, "We'll cross here as the sun falls behind the mountain.

The sun dipped behind the houses. A long black shadow began extending across the field. Grimface led the way, and the three men quickly covered the distance. They came to a stone wall and climbed over. A garden was laid out; flowers and vines were everywhere. Somewhere in the distance the gentle sound of singing came to their ears. A stairwell came into view and Grimface led the way. He froze. "I must wait here and prepare. It is time you made good on your boasting. Kill the guards and let us have access."

Benhargan positioned himself. Bulvife drew back his string. Both men let loose three arrows each. Six men fell silently to the garden below. Benhargan pointed and Bulvife took three more arrows and notched one. A guard came around the corner, a wooden shaft sunk into his chest, and he crumpled to the ground. Benhargan moved along the ledge and scaled the roof. He motioned for Bulvife to follow. Grimface stayed in the shadows.

Over the roof, ten men stood around a fire and cooking pot. Benhargan motioned at the targets, Bulvife drew back his string. This time eight men died quickly and two were left looking in shock at what had happened. Before they could let out a peep, Bulvife and Benhargan silenced them with their blades. They moved into the villa and skulked from room to room. When they were sure no more guards roamed free, they fetched Grimface.

Silently the three men scaled the roof and dropped down through a skylight into a fountain room. The singing they had heard became louder. Benhargan turned to Grimface, "Is the singing magic?" Grimface made no acknowledgement. Benhargan growled, "Then don't answer me."

Bulvife stopped and pointed into the hall; candlelight flickered and came toward them. He drew his blade and moved to the side of the room. Benhargan moved opposite. Grimface stood in the middle as if frozen. A darkly skinned blond woman came into the room. She sang with such a voice as to make the karibu weep with joy. In her hand was a brass candelabra with six white candles. She stopped and looked at Benhargan and Bulvife and smiled so sweetly as to make a man cut his own wrist by her look. She then glanced at Grimface and sang a few delightful notes. Grim turned to Benhargan and used his magic, moving him across the room and smashing him against Bulvife. Both Bulvife and Benhargan were pressed together, and a great weight forced their arms down. And yet, she sang. She came to Grimface and caressed his beardless face, then moved toward Bulvife and Benhargan. She lay hands on them, feeling their muscular arms and legs then she took Benhargan's weapons and set them on the floor. She then took Bulvife's knife and placed it against Benhargan's neck and sang.

Benhargan tried to move, but he was held fast. His muscles bulged, and his face turned red with the effort and yet he was immovable. The blade was against his neck, and he leered at the witch with malice and rage, though he was powerless to stop her. He just hoped that in the afterlife, Crom would let him have her as his plaything, for her beauty was undeniable. She smiled as she sang. The singing stopped and her eyes bulged. Benhargan sprang like an arrow away. Bulvife did the same. The two men scooped up their weapons and stood on either side as they watched Grimface garroting the she-devil. Her heavenly voice was now silenced, and her arms flapped like a goose on a string. In a matter of seconds, she fell limp and Grimface let her corpse collapse to the floor.

"What happened," demanded Benhargan.

Grimface cocked his head, "I can't hear what you're saying," He removed some wax covered cloth from his ears. "I had to keep her magic from infecting me, while I let her think she had control of me." He dropped the cloth to the floor. "Now..." reaching down he removed the woman's necklace and held it in his hand. "Here it is," he said. "Now, bear with me as I do what hasn't been done in a thousand years." Kneeling down he laid out the pieces of the amulet. He positioned them so they fit together. A flash of blue light filled the room and the edges spontaneously welded together. The seams glowed red for a moment then cooled. "We are almost done."

They quickly escaped the villa and maneuvered through the city streets. They arrived at the home of Grimface's friend, and he led them down into the basement and a broken wall that led to the sewers. The three men made their way past the city wall and out into the valley.

"Now where?" Bulvife said.

Grimface glanced over his shoulder at the coming moonlight, "To destroy Ottin'bar of course."

They traveled all night and by dawn were approaching the frontier hill fort of Baumont. Wooden palisades surrounded mud-brick buildings and timber framed shacks. A narrow wooden gate allowed entrance and exit, and a crowd of traders, travelers and hunters were gathered there.

"Greetings travelers, do you come to make trade?" a large man with a long black beard said.

"News from the frontier is what we seek," Benhargan looked the man in the eye.

Black beard became uncomfortable and took a step back, "None can get past Tohk, for there is an army moving along the border between Shem and Koth."

"What sort of army?" Bulvife knelt down on one knee and picked at some long grass.

"It is said that a wizard commands an army of the dead. He is making for Asgakin to lay siege to the city."

Grimface made no expression, "Army of the dead? Explain."

"I can't, I did not see it with mine own eyes. A man who was here yesterday made claim, but he has gone to the west."

"Is there anyone who is selling horses here," Grimface asked.

"Yes, see Gambi ben Hoy, he has sturdy mounts and is willing to sell."

"Where do we find this Gambi ben Hoy?" Grimface said.

The man pointed toward a round hut outside the fort, "He lives there," said the man.

They made their way to the hut. "You inside," Grimface called.

A thin, short and balding man stepped out. "I am Gambi ben Hoy," he said.

"We wish to purchase mounts from you. How much?" Benhargan stated.

Gambi scratched his chin and looked at the three men. "None of you look as if you have two brass coins to spit on."

"How much?" Grimface calmly said.

"Well, for you, three brass ingots...each. Then you can choose what horse you want from my herd."

"What if I cut your head off and we take what we want?" Benhargan hissed.

"Not a common bit of haggling, but I'll play. Two brass ingots and a day's labor?"

Benhargan's hand hovered at the hilt of his sword. Grimface stated, "How about this?" He pulled forth from the recesses of his robe five gems all different colors. He put them into the hand of Gambi and smiled. Gambi looked confused for a moment then grinned, "Yes, yes, let me show you the herd. Take which ones you want." His eyes did not leave the gems.

"Bring us blankets and halters and we will leave you to ogle your treasure," Grimface said as he dismissed the man. Gambi did as he was asked, and the three men were soon on their way south.

They traveled all day and into the night. The dirt road cut through farms and fields, some populated with wandering herdsmen. At one-point Grimface stopped and insisted that Benhargan and Bulvife eat a biscuit he was carrying in a satchel. The item was sweet, and Bulvife felt his blood rush. Benhargan's eyes widened.

"What was this we've all eaten?" Benhargan said.

Grimface looked back and smiled, "Tuti cakes," is all he stated.

They rode until false dawn when Grimface began walking his horse. Benhargan and Bulvife did likewise. Coming over a rise Benhargan could see a grove of trees. His eyesight caught the movement of men. "Movement ahead," he whispered.

"I see them too," Bulvife stated. "Grim, you hold the horses, Benhargan and I will see what is going on.

Benhargan moved silently and swiftly. He moved into the tree line and listened. The sound of men moving through the underbrush was apparent. He motioned for Bulvife to advance, and he notched an arrow. Bulvife maneuvered through the thicket. A subtle gasp could be heard, then silence. Bulvife returned carrying a body. Silently they carried the corpse through the brush back to Grimface.

"What have you here?" Grimface said.

Bulvife laid the body down face up, "Sure as the man at the fort told, it is the face of death." The body had a skeletal face, white with a rictus grin.

"Evil magic is afoot," Benhargan said looking about.

Grimface bent down. From his pouch he produced a circlet that glowed a purplish color. He held it near the face of the corps. "Ah," he said and pulled up on the face revealing another face underneath. "A mask. No wonder simple minds thought Ottin'bar's ranks were filled with the walking dead."

"He is a Vanir mercenary," Bulvife stated.

Grimface looked at his companions, "Let us find the camp of these jackals."

They circled around the grove of trees and moved up a hill. As they came over the hill a thousand campfires blazed ahead of them. Benhargan knelt and drew a symbol in the dirt. Bulvife grunted his agreement, "Ten thousand men to be sure." The two men turned to Grimface.

He took in a deep breath. "Tomorrow, we will place ourselves between them and the city. I will need you two by my side."

"We will send many of them to the embrace of their gods before the day is done," Benhargan stated.

"Our quivers will be empty, and the thirst of our blades for blood sated by the time we are felled!" Bulvife huffed.

"No," Grimface began looking at the stand of small trees. He found a long straight sapling and pointed, "Cut it down, blunt and narrow the end." He sat down cross legged and removed the medallion. "I'll handle the bulk of the soldiers and Ottin'bar. This will require strong magic. The stragglers who get past me, you will have to deal with them, for if I fall, the might of his army will crash down upon you. But, if I live, that same army will smash around us like waves on the jagged rocks of Tara."

"Crom will be pleased," Bulvife stated.

A crimson dawn welcomed all. Four columns five men wide trailed for miles. Cavalry were at the front on either side like wings of a hawk. At the head was a man on horseback carrying a staff tipped with something golden and studded with gems. Grimface glanced behind;

the city walls of Kothbah were manned by soldiers with sword and spear, and archers with their bows at the ready. "Prepare yourselves," he said to Benhargan and Bulvife. "Those city dwellers will be of little use to us in this fight."

The column grew larger as they approached. At a hundred yards out Ottin'bar held up his staff and the march halted. He rode out a few hundred feet and looked upon the two barbarians and the mystic with surprise and contempt. "What is this?" he said loudly. "Ants baring the path of the elephant?"

Grimface kept his own staff hidden behind his back. "Your end is at hand Ottin'bar ben Ghul," he shouted. "You think your army is an elephant? My army of three is all that stands in your way. Come hither and find why an ant can devour the pachyderm."

Ottin'bar scoffed and shook his head, "I will order your deaths as easily as I did the death of your family, and your village, and your king. I will oblige you in this, for Set wills it to be." He turned and rode back to his line.

"Be ready. Do not stray more than twenty paces to either side," Grimface told his companions.

Ottin'bar motioned with his staff and archers rushed to the front. They lined up twenty to a line and ten lines deep. They planted arrows into the ground, notched one, and drew back. Ottin yelled, and the volley was loosed.

Grimface pulled the staff from behind his back, held it aloft and chanted in an unworldly tone. The arrows landed everywhere but into the three men. Ottin'bar became enraged and ordered another volley. These arrows also missed their marks. Again, the sky darkened with arrows and again all missed. Ottin called up a hundred infantry and sent them toward Grimface. They walked a hundred feet then broke into a charge. They bore down on the three men. Benhargan and Bulvife stood with arrows at the ready. When the infantry were sixty feet away, Benhargan and Bulvife let fly; twelve of the hundred soldiers fell to the dust. The core of the charge struck an invisible force and man after man fell and tripped over one another. A dozen men came around the sides and Bulvife and Benhargan took sword in hand and went to work. Blades clashed and blood soaked into the ground. Twelve soldiers lay prone while Benhargan and Bulvife laid out more arrows to use. The remaining soldiers struggled to get up then screamed as their skin turned black and cracked; incinerated in place.

Ottin'bar shouted and motioned with his staff. His army began moving forward. Dust rose and, in the sky, carrion birds cried out for the feast yet to be. Grimface raised his staff and sang so sweetly that the very sky shone with white light and thunder. The first line of men fell, as did the second, and then the third. From the sides came the cavalry in a charge. The ground shook and the dust filled the air obscuring the advancing army. As before the middle column smashed into some unseen force as horse with rider were laid low. The two Cimmerians let fly their arrows bringing down both mount and man. Around the edges twelve horsemen came at Grimface. Benhargan cut six riders from their horses, his tremendous battle shout filling the air. Bulvife nimbly dodged this way and that, his sword a blur of thrust and parry. Two horses escaped and fled, their cries of fear echoing behind them. Soon bodies were in heaps to the sides. The rest of the army was a hundred feet from them and advancing. Spears were thrown, and twenty-foot-long javelins were put out front.

"This will be a glorious death," shouted Benhargan.

Bulvife fired his remaining arrows. The missiles struck shields and men.

Ottin'bar began to sing and though there were no clouds, the sky darkened. At the front of Ottin's army dark black beasts twice the size of men appeared. They rushed at Grimface whose voice carried a note of charm and longing. The monsters were enveloped by a swirling light and vanished in a puff of white smoke. The army reached them, as Ottin'bar leapt from his horse and brought his staff down at Grimface.

Grimface reached out with his hand and seized the aggressor's staff and stripped him of his weapon in one move. Ottin'bar fell to the ground and rolled to his feet. A blade came to his hand and he lunged at the back of Grimface. Benhargan and Bulvife latched on to Ottin and held him fast. Grimface's tune changed and Bulvife and Benhargan felt tears come to their eyes. Hands reached from the dirt and latched onto the legs of the army. From the earth came horrors, twisted manlike shapes. Soldiers screamed in terror and many who had yet to be set upon fled. The darkness fell away and the creatures rend all those living beings limb from limb. When the screaming stopped, more than ten thousand men-at-arms littered the ground, torn apart.

Grimface silenced and let his staff down. He turned to Ottin'bar, "Not since the great flood of Huron valley has such things come to pass. You stole from me, my wife and children, mother, brothers, sisters, and father. You took my king and like a thief in the night his kingdom. You acquired dark magic and relics, and thought your future made anew." He raised the staff, "Your sacred name is known to me, and I have the power to undo you. On this day of your greatest triumph, I have stolen your future. Now, I consign you to eternal damnation, and for all the rest of your living day shall be spent in bondage Ottin'bar Abel ben Garza." He sang, and Benhargan and Bulvife fell to the side with such hatred in their hearts that their eyes saw only red. Ottin'bar screamed, raised his hands then shrank. He grew smaller, and smaller, until he was hidden within his robe. Grimface reached down and pulled the garment away to reveal a monkey. He quickly locked a collar on it with a long golden chain. "Death is not a punishment enough for you. Welcome to your new life," he smiled.

Turning to Benhargan and Bulvife he handed the two barbarians Ottin'bar's staff, "You will need to replace this whence you got it. The curse upon your heads will be lifted then."

Benhargan looked over the carnage. Atop the heaps of bodies were the ravenous birds. From the surrounding hills came the jackals and dogs to feast upon the carrion. He turned back to the city. The walls were vacant now, abandoned by the fearful. "I have never seen anything like this," he stated.

Bulvife got to his feet, "Nor I." He looked at Grimface, "So, he butchered your family and king?"

"He and his army did many, many years ago."

"What of our treasure?" Benhargan said.

Grimface looked weary. He staggered but propped himself with his staff. "It is carried at the rear with the luggage. There you will find more than a kingdoms wealth. Take it, take it all," he said. "I know you will use it to sate your base lust and desires." He chuckled, "I would follow you and do the same, but I must now take this amulet and return it to its resting place, a promise I made long ago."

Bulvife nodded, "But that staff is powerful. Surely you could use it to your own ends?"

"Just when I thought you were smarter than a rock, you prove me wrong barbarian. No man can wield this power for long. It will bend and twist the common man and plunge his soul into darkness. I must now put it where none can find it again, whence it came where the waters devoured its maker."

"I understand. Such a thing would only make fiends into kings," Bulvife looked thoughtful.

"Yes, perhaps you are not as dumb as you look," Grimface chuckled.

"Once we have hidden our treasure, and unloaded this curse we will follow you," Benhargan stated. "Leave word at the Green Jade Tavern and we will catch up."

Grimface staggered. "I must now rest. Help me get to the city and there I must sleep for several days. Perhaps this time you'll not let my rest be disturbed for want of cunny." He looked up at both men. "Don't worry, your treasure will be safe here, for none will approach for fear of the demons that will guard it."

The two Cimmerians helped Grimface toward the city. Bulvife glanced back at the carnage. Standing there with arms crossed towered a twenty-foot-tall demon. Its fire red eyes watched them as they left.

BOOK 2
The Ties that Bind

CHAPTER 1
REVELATIONS

GRIMFACE STOOD BALANCED on the prow of the rowboat at the center of a vast lake. In his hand he cradled the most powerful magic he'd ever known. Below him were the remains of his home, lost to the great flood so many years ago. There was no way for his rowers to know that he had seen more than a thousand winters, and there was no way for them to know, he was the last of his kind. Why should they know, for they were only common clay molded by some forgiving god, not learned in the ways of magic or earthly knowledge. He looked back at them; two simple fishermen, one older, one younger staring back with their oars in hand. He glanced back toward the V shaped valley in the far distance and remembered the glacial dam that reached to the sky. He gritted his teeth with anger at the thought of Ottin'bar's treachery at cracking the great frozen dam and inundating his home with a hundred feet of water. Grimface's eyes saddened, and he felt that he no longer belonged among the living; he prepared to step over. At last, he could rest with his family, his kind, long since melted into the mud of this massive lake.

"Boats," the older fishermen said.

"Ten at least," the younger said.

Turning to look, Grimface could see them on the horizon. Indeed, there were at least ten boats, ladened with armed men. He closed his eyes and a vision flashed before his sight. "Give me your fishing twine," he said. He took the twine and looped it through the amulet. "Give me that cork," He pointed and received the punkie wood. "Keep an eye on those boats." He secured the long string to the light wood and the amulet. Reaching into a chum bucket he pulled out a hunk of stinking bait and fed it through a hole in the amulet, then lowered it into the water. The bob dunked once, then again, and finally vanished. Saying a few words, he turned and returned to the bow and sat. "If you value your lives, you'd better row like heroes," he said to them.

They rowed for the better part of an hour. It was no good, the enemy closed on them. Grimface staggered toward the aft of the boat. Once there, he raised his hands and began to sing. The water vibrated and soon a white fog rose from the waters. In a matter of seconds, the pursuing boats were lost in the mist. He turned back and made his way to the prow and sat again.

"Who are they?" the one fisherman said.

"Warriors sent by a prince to capture me," Grimface said. "Make no mistake, if you are thinking of turning this boat about, they will cut your throats before any bounty is paid to you." The two men looked at each other and rowed harder.

Soon the stony shore was visible. Scrubs and pine trees a dozen feet from the beach filled the backdrop. The sound of the pursuing men was growing louder behind them. "If you don't mind my asking," one of the fishermen said, "you're a wizard?"

Grimface almost smiled, "Of a sort."

"Then, can you endow us with some super strength so we can out pace those rascals?"

"It doesn't work like that. I don't have the proper materials to do such a thing here. If I had some promuda root, and some ginga leaves, and maybe the liver of a falcon, I might whip something up."

"Pity," said the fishermen as he strained at the oar.

The pursuers broke through the fog. They were scattered about, but still heading toward Grimface and the shore. Grimface turned toward the shore, and something caught his eye that made him laugh. He sat back facing the rowers. "You can take heart now."

"Why is that wizard?" one said.

"There are two ferocious beasts on the shore."

The two fishermen looked concerned, "How is that going to help us?" the other said.

"It might not," Grimface shrugged. "Then again, it might do us well."

The boat rammed into the shore and the three men jumped out. Grimface pointed into the dense forest. "Keep to the woods. Go that way, and from time to time climb a tree. If you see Mundu Peak," he again pointed, "You will be heading in the right direction."

"What about you?" the older of the two men asked.

"I'll stay here and meet my destiny."

"What of the beasts," the younger said.

"I have faith they will leave you alone. Now go." The two fishermen ran into the woods even as the enemy boats came within arrow distance.

"Give us the amulet," shouted a great hairy beast of a man.

"It is here for the taking," Grimface said. Under his breath he spoke, "and let my old eyes have seen true, and these beasts lurk now with me."

The man in the lead boat shouted, "When we are done, only your bones will tell of the tale." Three of the boats slammed into the sand and a dozen armed soldiers leapt to the shore. "Don't let him sing," a man with a prefect's helmet commanded.

Grimface stepped back. "I have no need to sing for you," he calmly said. "But I will pray for you."

The man scoffed. "Your boasting will not save you now." He stepped forward and was covered in blood. His head fell from its place to the shore as Benhargan ran headlong into the other soldiers. His battle cry shook the ground as he swung his brass blade from body to body. Arrows flew past Grimface into the approaching rowers. Men in the boats cried out as arrow after arrow struck them.

"It's an ambush," a man in a feathered helmet shouted. "Retreat back out into the water!"

The dozen men on shore were put to slaughter, and Benhargan called to the fleeing men, "Who bore you? City dwellers, cowards flee from honest fight!" He turned to face Grimface, "And you? What excuse do you give for not sending word sooner of your travel?"

Grimface calmly smiled. "It was that word that brought those men down upon me I suspect." He heard Bulvife come from the bushes, "And you two are welcome figures to be sure."

"We could take that rowboat and pursue them," Bulvife said.

"To what end?" Grimface shook his head.

"To ensure that none report back to... to whomever."

"It doesn't matter." Grimface clasped hands with the two barbarians. "How is it that you came to be here on this shore?"

"We were on our way to the village you described," Benhargan said, "when we discovered this massive lake in our way."

"The highway you pointed us to, ended at the lake's edge," Bulvife stated as he notched an arrow. "So, we followed the shoreline and that led us here."

"I'm still amazed at the power of the gods," Grimface said.

Benhargan looked down at Grimface, "and I'm still amazed that you are not dead."

"Shall we take this boat?" Bulvife walked over to it.

"The village is two days from here through the woods. We have a better chance at getting there if we do that," Grimface said.

Bulvife leaned against the side of the boat. "We've only had some greasy game hare these past few days. Some bull-deer would do us well."

Grimface nodded. "Dwarf white deer roam these woods. They make for good roasting."

"Then by foot we travel," Benhargan grunted, "and, to hell with this boat." He grabbed it by the bow and pulled it up on shore and shoved it into the woods. "Those fools, if they return will be confused when they see all the shore is as empty as their heads. If they do come back, this will buy us some time."

Grimface turned and said over his shoulder, "Follow barbarians, and we shall make camp at the home of Shelb, the goddess of lust!"

"I like this land already," Bulvife said.

"They had better pray that they have enough women and food to keep me sated," Benhargan stated, "Or, there will be much weeping for the carnage." He quickened his pace.

The crumbling walls of the temple came into view. Birds swarmed from its towers, and game moved in and out of its corridors. Benhargan sniffed the air, "No people."

"No," Grimface said. "They've all been gone for many years now."

"Where is this food and women you promised?"

"I didn't promise you those things. You just assumed there would be food and women. You made a bad assumption."

"It is unwise to provoke me," Benhargan said through clenched teeth.

Grimface almost chuckled at the foolish man. "At one time there were women and feasts to put all that you've enjoyed to shame."

Bulvife kept his arrow notched while scanning the forest. "What happened here?"

"The end of civilization. Once this place was filled with people, food, harmony and magic. Long ago it was destroyed." He approached a pyramidal archway. "Enter and meet the ghosts of my past."

It took little time for Bulvife and Benhargan to find enough game to feed them. Grimface made a fire in the main hall, and they roasted meat and talked late into the night. They took turns keeping watch,

Grimface taking the last. Small frogs and birds filled the dark night with croaking and chirping, and in the distance the growl of a large cat echoed. Bulvife drifted off to sleep. Benhargan slumped by the fire and slept with one eyelid parted. Grimface walked about the hall.

Bulvife woke. It was strangely quiet. The fire was only red coals. He could see the outline of a man in the darkness. Getting to his feet, Bulvife moved silently toward the figure. He stopped and watched. It was Grimface, and he held a bowl of something at the base of a weathered statue. "It has been long since I spoke your name," Grimface softly said. "I bring a sacrifice, my own blood and the paste of the sacred mushroom." He knelt down and placed the bowl at the foot of the statue. "I have served you nigh on ten centuries, and I ask you, when will my time to rest come?"

Like the branches of a tree, blue crackling fingers of energy came from the statue and touched Grimface about the head and upper torso. His body went rigid, and he fell back. The blue forked energy vanished. Bulvife approached. The bowl was empty, and Grimface unconscious.

"What did the fool do now?" Benhargan said coming up behind Bulvife.

"I'm not sure, but it is true that he's not of this world."

Benhargan bent down and grabbed Grimface by the legs. "Take him by the arms and let's bring him by the fire." They carried Grimface to the fire. Benhargan put some wood in the coals and blew into the pit. Long yellow flames illuminated the room.

"He is a strange shade of white," Bulvife stated.

"With any luck, he's dead," Benhargan said.

"For him or us?"

"Maybe both."

Grimface screamed out. Bulvife ran to where he lay, "What is it?"

Sitting up Grimface shook with some fever. "The roar, no beast can escape it!"

"Quiet him before those mercenaries come to find us," Benhargan said as he removed his sword from its scabbard.

"The dragon, the beast knows," Grimface stammered, "the demons, by all holy Mir the demons claw at my soul." His eyes closed and sweat poured from his face. "The water, I must have it, the cool water." Bulvife retrieved his water-skin and gave Grimface a drink. "Thank the gods, thank the gods..." he said before falling unconscious again.

Hours passed as Benhargan paced, and Bulvife attended Grimface. Finally, just as the darkness of night fell again, Grimface struggled to his feet. He looked about as if unsure where he was.

"We thought you were going to die," Benhargan said. "I was wondering on what to do with your hide."

Grimface drank deeply from the water-skin then sat down. "My god, showed me a vision of things to come."

"And you don't want to tell Benhargan that he weds a camel? I can understand that" Bulvife stated.

Benhargan grunted, "We've wasted a day here and a night, and we must spend another night? It is a fool's rest with those soldiers looking for us."

"There is a change coming to the world. An island will vanish, a race scattered to the winds. A forest will die, and a grassland will turn to sand." Grimface looked around. "Where is Benhargan's wine skin?" He found it, pulled the cork and drank for a long while. "Those soldiers were sent to get the amulet, but by their folly drove me into the hands of Shelb. They want the amulet so their master can stop these things. But those spirits that mark our destiny are far more powerful than that amulet." He drank again.

"How will he get it with it resting at the bottom of this lake?" Benhargan said.

Grimface looked uncomfortable, "It is not at the bottom of the lake."

"What?" Bulvife said.

"It has a powerful draw to men. The enemy was bearing down on me, if I was to release it...what if I needed it again..." He seemed confused, lost in thought. "Yes, it was the vision, the one on the boat. It couldn't be lost, not now."

"What if the other gets it?" Benhargan folded his arms.

Grimface shrugged. "My ancestors forged it as a gift to a god-king. He used it benevolently to make rivers, forests of fruit trees, honey hives as large as termite mounds. With a wave of the amulet, fields of yellow grain waved in the wind from horizon to horizon, and the bread, beer, and wine flowed from presses and amphora like rain from a storm."

"All well and good, but what of the men who are not god-kings?" Bulvife stated.

"As it has affected me, it will affect them too. None will willingly surrender the gift." Grimface looked toward the lake.

"You will." Benhargan said. "And, in the darkness we will find it and send it to the bottom of the lake."

Grimface took a rabbit leg and tore some flesh from it. "You see things in such simple terms."

"And you in such complex ways," Benhargan chided him.

"There is a part of my vision that I haven't told you yet. In my haste I left the amulet tied to a string that was tied to a bob of cork. A lake creature has eaten the amulet, and the beast was caught in a fisherman's net. Even now, the amulet, string and bob will be found by a man not far from here. And, as the world will be changed, so will our lives."

"I wish you would just say what's going to happen," Benhargan said.

"Or at least -," a sound echoed through the hall, armor and men were coming. "Perhaps, this discussion can wait. We've been found," Bulvife quietly stated as he notched an arrow.

CHAPTER 2
RUIN'S LOST LOVES

THE ENEMY WAS QUIET, but rangers know the sounds of sloppy stealth. Mercenaries were not far off, merely beyond the walls of the main temple hall. Grimface pulled at Bulvife's arm, "This way. These vermin will know not how we escaped." He led the way toward the statue. To one side he pulled at a clump of debris then moved toward the back of the pedestal. Sliding open a compartment, he exposed a cleverly hidden passageway. "Those fools will find our hot fire, but no three idiots warming beside it."

They slipped into the passage, Grimface closed the door, and they went down a carved stone staircase. A subtle blue glow emanated from the walls illuminating their path. At the bottom he stopped. A worn pathway led down a corridor illuminated in green. "Not down that passage," Grimface said and led them down a tunnel lined with the blue glowing stone.

"What is down that way?" Bulvife looked back.

"Only confusion and death," Grimface stated.

"What makes these rocks so bright," Benhargan said.

"The rocks do not glow, but what grows on them does. The blue moss only grows toward the open air, and that is how the priests of old would find their way out of these caverns of the dead. Those who did not know the secret would do what you were about to do and follow the wrong path."

Bulvife became aware that stacked along the walls were bones. Skulls, arms, legs, spines, all stacked like cordwood on either side. From time to time he would see the empty sockets of a skull pass by and he wondered what had brought these soul's their deaths. A draft could be felt, and it built in strength. Bulvife could smell the earth and greenwoods ahead. The sound of running water greeted his ears and soon all three men found themselves on a ledge overlooking a waterfall and a river.

"When I was a young man," Grimface began, "a bridge traversed this crevasse. I crossed it many times on my way home from the temple." He again led the way down a narrow ledge toward the river. "The flesh eaters used to prowl these woods and streams. They feared we priests, knowing what demons we could summon, but sometimes -," he gave a sardonic chuckled, "one of our kind would fall victim."

At the base Grimface found misshaped boulders, some as large as the temple hall, perched atop smaller stones. The crystal-clear waters of the river drove around them, and in some places cut a hole through the middle of several boulders. It was no easy matter for Grimface to pick his way across spans of water, over lumps of stone, and under massive blocks held aloft by smaller more fragile stones. Once on the other side he stopped and dabbed his scarf in the cool water. Wiping his neck with it, he looked up at the switchback path from which they had come. "Someone knows of that cavern, or that path would not have remained so clean," he said.

"Who cares," growled Benhargan, "let's get to that fishmonger."

Bulvife moved ahead, and vanished into the woods, then came back. "No sign of recent travel this way."

"Good, for that is the way we need to go," Grimface said.

The air carried a freshness about it. From time-to-time Grimface would inhale deeply, and as if in ecstasy would exhale with satisfaction.

Benhargan kept an eye on their flank as they moved over fallen tree trunks, and around massive trees that reached into the sky. As Bulvife passed one of the mammoth arbors, he commented, "More than a hundred cubits at the base."

Grimface laughed, "These were merely children when I was swept away. Now, these Gocolana trees scratch the clouds. When I was young, a city was amongst these timbers high up in the branches. The mature trees stop growing at nearly a thousand feet high."

"Whose feet," Bulvife said.

Benhargan chuckled, "You two chatter like old women with a baby!" He approached and walked alongside Grimface. "I've seen the great red trees by Herot. It is true that these are much larger."

"Yes. You could stack five or ten of the tallest red trees to match the height of a Gocolana tree." The path forked. Grimface took the path that led through one of the giant trees. At some point in the past the arbor had forked then grown back together fifty feet up. Now it looked as if it were standing on two stout legs. A strange sound echoed through the forest and Grimface stopped.

"I've never heard an animal that makes such a sound," Benhargan said.

"The uberoo," Grimface laughed. "I've not heard that sound for a thousand years." He wound his way off the trail and between giant green ferns that spread out over the peaty ground. "Come," was all he said.

As they came around a dense clump of undergrowth Benhargan pulled his sword. A creature that resembled a bear but stood three times as tall. It had a massive head, but the muzzle was shorter. Its dark green and brown eyes were looking at a fern and Benhargan motioned for Bulvife to prepare an arrow. Grimface held up his hand, "No need for such," and he walked up to the monster and laid his hand on it.

The creature moved extremely slowly as it turned its head to look down at Grimface, Benhargan, and Bulvife. Even its blinking was extremely slow. "What manner of monster is this," Benhargan said amazed.

"My people called it by its true name, uberoo." Grimface petted it as he smiled broadly. "They are the children of the forest. Mostly they live in the high trees, but sometimes they come down to eat the lush ferns. Gentles are these creatures, but they are not good to hunt or eat for their flesh is bitter, and poisonous. It is one of the two reasons why most predators steer clear of them."

"Look what we have here boys," the deep voice of a man erupted.

Benhargan pulled his sword, but Grimface laid his hand on his forearm. "Wait."

"Why do you interfere," Benhargan grunted.

"Stay your weapons and stand close to the uberoo," Grimface said.

Mercenaries came from all sides. One large man with a feathered helmet and a round shield approached. "You've given us a pretty chase, but it's at an end," he said. "Throw down your weapons and we'll finish you quickly. Don't, and it will go hard for you."

"You stink of perfume, and like a whore, you'll sing at the end of my weapon," Benhargan challenged.

"He thinks he's a hero," the man said. "We'll save something for you that's creative." He pointed at the twenty troops who surrounded the three men. "There is nowhere for you to go. When we're done with you, we'll kill that beast too."

Grimface looked at Benhargan and Bulvife, "Sometimes forethought is our best ally, not strength of arms," he said. "While the uberoo is gentle, slow, and toxic to eat, they have a strange ability to call upon the jhut when they are threatened."

"What is a jhut?" Benhargan said.

"A creature that man fears in this forest, for the jhut loves the taste of human flesh," Grimface stated. "Watch."

Several of the mercenaries screamed as a dozen large black hairy beasts came forth. They resembled lions, but twice as big with black fur and razor-sharp tusks. The creatures hit the men deliberately at three points and panic ensued. "What are they!" screamed one man who swung his sword to no avail. Two men were disemboweled, two more dismembered, and three dragged into the ferns screaming until silenced.

Benhargan's veins bulged as he clenched his sword. Grimface kept his hand on Benhargan's arm. "Do not hunger for your own death so readily. We are quite safe here. The one thing a jhut does not like, and even fears is the uberoo. None of them will approach us as long as we stand here." Blood stained the ground all around as soldiers tried to defend. Even well-placed stabs by sword or dagger were little more than pin pricks to the creatures who devoured their prey. In less than five minutes, all the aggressors were slaughtered, their torn and bloody flesh littering the green vegetation.

The creatures stayed for an hour while they happily crunched bones and dug meat from armor. A few times the beasts approached the uberoo, but an acrid smell filled the air and the jhut's melted into the shadows of the forest and were gone. "They are stealthier than we are," Bulvife said surprised.

"And how is it those soldiers found us so fast?" Benhargan demanded.

Grimface nodded his head, "If an enemy haunts your steps, it is good to exercise him from your presence," he said.

"You did this?" Benhargan grunted the realization hitting him.

"Yes barbarian. I smelled the uberoo when we were on the cliff. I led those soldiers here. You would do well to think one or two steps ahead too."

Bulvife laughed, "Only in a battle," he said.

Benhargan said nothing and continued to watch the woods.

"What do you see...or hear," Bulvife said.

"Nothing," Benhargan stated. "That's what worries me."

"The jhut have sated their want for flesh and will bother us no more today. Let us now move unmolested to our destination." Grimface left the side of the uberoo and quickly found the trail. From there he led the way through the woods to a valley, then to a village beside the lake.

The water in the lake was dark blue. From their approach the village seemed a large encampment. Hundreds of huts and lodges were scattered about, and many boats bobbed up and down in the small cove. A pack of wild dogs were gorging themselves at the garbage pit, while women used stones to crush roots and nuts. The stench of fish hung in the air, and Grimface maneuvered between the drying racks that contained the flayed creatures. Near the shore he found a group of old men sitting around a fire pit. "Grandfather, who here caught a big fish that held in its guts a hunk of metal?"

One old man stood, "I found the metal. It spoke to me, and I carried it to the place it spoke of."

Grimface looked surprised, "Spoke to you?"

"Yes. It called me to the spot where I laid out my nets. It told me which fish to harvest that contained it within." The old man sat down again. "It spoke of you too, and how you forged it anew."

"Where did it say you should take it?"

The old man shrugged his shoulders, "To the witch who lives in the old cliff city. I left last night and returned this morning. She told me that a wizard would come to see me and that those who pursue you are from the island of Antitis far to the west."

"Anything more," Grimface said.

The old man smiled a toothless grin, "The changeling will be born, and Antitis will fall." The old man poked at the fire with a stick.

"Where is this witch?" Grimface looked worried.

The old man took the stick with its flaming end and pointed south. "There, where the ruins of the carved city are. She still lives there and speaks of things yet to pass."

"Who is this witch?" Benhargan demanded to know.

Grimface shrugged his shoulders. "I did not see this in my vision. But, if she has the amulet, we need to go there." He raised his hand to the old man, "Bless you for your part in this task," he said. The man shuddered once then poked at the fire again.

Grimface followed the shoreline to where several boats were beached. A young man stood mending a net as Grimface pointed at a boat. "We'll take that one," he declared.

"Wait a minute!" The young man said coming to his feet.

Grimface waved his hand, "Sleep," he said, and the man promptly sat down and closed his eyes. He turned to Benhargan and Bulvife, "push us out into the water and make sail. We have a hard bit of rowing to accomplish. If we're lucky, we will be at the foot of the city by dark."

A stout wind gathered as they put up the sail and stowed the oars. The small boat cut across the glassy lake toward a set of high ridges for most of the day. As the ridges grew into tall cliffs, Benhargan began roaming the boat like a caged animal. "There is nothing to do on this blasted boat," he complained.

Grimface angled the rudder and gave Benhargan a disapproving look, "Meditate, contemplate, or pray to your god for a while."

"My nature is to do battle and lay low armies. I am unaccustomed to those things you ask. If you wanted me to not complain, you should have brought some women with us then I'd be occupied!"

Bulvife sat at the bow, his sword across his lap watching the approaching cliffs. "The rocks are unnatural. They've been shaped," he said. "I feel anxious as Benhargan, but I cannot take my eyes from those cliffs."

Benhargan stormed to the prow and gazed out for a minute. "Not only are those cliffs carved into dwellings, but they are also occupied too." He pointed at some white smoke coming from a high ledge. "I think that window is five hundred feet above the lake."

Grimface angled the boat toward a set of long shadows extending into the lake. "Once those dwellings would have been teaming with caravans, traders, and people, but they should be as empty as Benhargan's head."

Bulvife chuckled, "Nothing can be that empty."

"Shut up you both, you're disturbing my watch," Benhargan said as he continued to watch the cliffs with intense interest.

"What is it you see there?" Grimface said.

"A shadowy figure came out onto the ledge from where the smoke is and looked out then retreated back inside." He looked at Grimface, "We should expect a reception."

The boat was only three hundred yards away from the cliffs. They could now see the resplendent structures, temples, villas, shops, all faced with columns, gables, friezes, carved statues, and scrolling. The sun was going down, and shadows abounded, but the stone shone like polished yellow gold. All along the stonework were twinkling gems, and every now and again, lines of gold and silver appeared crisscrossing along the walls. Grimface steered the boat toward a row of a hundred columns that rose from the water. "Drop the sail. From here we row," he said.

Benhargan and Bulvife rowed as they fell into the shadow of the cliff. Grimface angled the boat between the columns and gave the command to stop. The boat bumped against the walls, and he spoke, "We're here. Climb into that window and secure the boat."

Bulvife looked and saw a window twenty feet wide and ten feet high. He took the bow rope and slipped into the darkness. The rope came taunt, and he appeared in the opening again. "It's secured. I tied it to a stone table."

Grimface and Benhargan followed Bulvife. Bluish light emanated from the walls and floor. Grimface then led them to a stairwell, and they began the climb upward. At every landing he stopped and listened then moved up again. Benhargan kept trying to run past, but Grimface would put his arm out and shake his head. Benhargan remained anxious as they moved through villas, and temples, all filled with the low light of the bluish glow. No sign of habitation remained, no plates, no comforts, no smells.

As they rose to the next level, the smell of food hit the three men hard. Rich and spiced, whatever it was smelled delicious. They came down a hallway and Grimface held up his hand. The scent was strong here. The doorway was lit with the glow of firelight. He looked inside and to his surprise a long stone table set with four placements, candles, and food were piled high. "Stay here," he said and went inside.

He looked about the room. Several doorways gave access. He approached the table.

"You've come a long way," a woman's voice said.

Grimface turned and took a step back. He felt the blood drain from his face, and he thought for a moment he would pass out. She came into the room, her dress made from gossamer silk, nearly transparent. A circlet of gold was around her dark black hair. She came to the table and picked up a goblet of wine and drank some. "I did not know it would be you," she said. "But now that you are here, I have grim news to tell you, oh my brother."

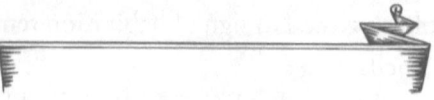

CHAPTER 3
PATH TO YAMEN

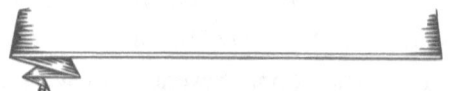

GRIMFACE APPROACHED the table. His hands visibly shook. "How...I mean..."

"The flood came without warning. I was trading in the lower levels of the city. A woman cried out from the upper balcony that a wall of water was rushing down the valley. I ran as fast as I could as the water smashed everything in its path." She brushed back her long hair and sat at the table. "The water crested just below this villa. All those below were washed away. The sound of thunder crashed all about and the cries of the souls being dragged off to their doom was deafening." She drank from the goblet. "Out of the two hundred thousand inhabitants, twenty of us survived; mostly women and children who were in the high homes." She looked forlorn, "They all moved away after the waters settled. I alone stayed."

"Why," Grimface asked.

"At the time it seemed pointless to wander. After all, the lake was a tomb and all that was our family was encased within. Why not stay and mourn?"

"Bulvife, Benhargan, come in," Grimface called. The two barbarians entered the room. "This is my sister Chalicha. Chali, these

two beasts are Cimmerians. They're from the far north, born and bred
in the wild. They've served me well in my vengeance against Ottin'bar."

She stood, "He's dead?"

"He's not exactly dead, but I'm sure he wishes he was." Grimface
came and sat at the table.

Benhargan approached, grabbed some meat and savagely tore into
it. "They say you are a witch?" Food flew from his mouth as he spoke.
"We were told that you have a metal trinket that a fisherman found."

She looked up at Benhargan, "I do have such a thing. The old
fisherman brought it to me, and I recognized it. It must have been at
the bottom of the lake for all these years; ancient and powerful. The
god king wielded it in my youth. He too is lost at the bottom of the
lake."

Grimface drank. "The fishmonger said you spoke of prophecy. That
I need to go to the island of Antitis."

She smiled. "I did. Much has happened in a thousand years since
you left. But I say to you it is not the King of Antitis that is at issue, it is
his son the prince."

Grimface took some food on a plate and took a bite. He savored
it for a moment as the lost memories of a thousand years rushed back,
then he spoke, "What of this vision you've had?"

"Soon, the land will buckle, and the Island of Antitis and its sisters
will be torn apart. The king of that land will need to evacuate his
people. Know this – the Antitian King's son seeks the power of the
God-King to add to his power. He says it is to hold back this doom.
The boy is ruthless, and equally stupid. Now he has magic in his hands
and his cruelty is spreading. He is most dangerous, for he commands
the Atlantean Pearl."

Bulvife wiped some wine from his lips, "How do you know these
things?"

Benhargan leaned over the table and eyed Chali like a prize. "Perhaps you'd like to entertain me for a while," he said with an amorous tone.

She dismissed him with a wave of her hand and the giant barbarian took a seat and looked askance. "I will do as you command," he mumbled and stared off into the distance. Bulvife also looked off with a blank stare.

Pouring more wine into her cup, Chali crossed her slender legs and drank from her goblet. "To answer the beast's question, I have visitors who come to hear of things to be. Recently, a man in a long gray robe came to visit me. I made him wait in the room below this one, and there he asked his questions. I looked into the mist of time and saw the end of his kingdom. But I also saw the prince and his cruel deeds..." she said.

Taking another helping, Grimface sat back, "So, the boy has the Pearl. Is that all?"

"No, the man in the robe then asked me of the amulet. I told him it had been lost a thousand years. He insisted that it was found and broken, then mended and now was close by." She giggled, "I dismissed him as easily as this brute," she pointed at Benhargan. "Once out in his boat he cursed at me for sending him way. Then, I felt it in my bones. Another of my kind was near. A few weeks later the old man brought me the amulet, and a day later you came." She stood and went to the fire. The glow of the flames made the gossamer dress vanish and her worldly assets emerged in pale shadow. "We and your brutes will go to Antitis and take the amulet."

"Why?" Grimface said.

"That prince has awoken a Kracken with his magic. It has laid waste to his enemies and destroys any boat leaving the island. He wants to keep his newfound power, and this amulet is the only thing that will ensure his control over nature. He moves even now to seize the throne for himself and displace his father. It will take us both to unseat him."

Grimface nodded his head. "That's why. It makes sense now –my vision." He drank some wine. "That's why I could not step off the boat or get rid of the amulet. The gods need me for one last blessed sacrifice. I trust after this; I will see my children again."

Chali smiled, "It is not you alone brother. It is my destiny too. We will face the foe together, and at last be reunited with our people."

Bulvife looked around, "What happened?"

Benhargan stood up. "What? Why am I still clothed?" His eyes fell on Chali again. "Mmm... you shall be mine this night." She waved her hand again and Benhargan and Bulvife again became passive.

"How do you put up with these creatures?"

Grimface glanced over at Bulvife and Benhargan, "They are smarter than boars, and twice as deadly," he said. "We will need them, and they will live, I've seen it."

She nodded her head. "Yes, but we won't."

The fire-red hue of the setting sun extended over the mountains. The reflection made it look as if the lake were a blaze with churning red coals. Benhargan stood on the veranda looking out at the water, his hands resting on the railing.

Grimface approached, "As a child I loved the sunrise. I could actually feel it in my chest while the light reflected through the ice walls. The valley would be awash with red, orange and pink."

Benhargan stared out at the horizon. "Your people are better off with your god. We mortals do not need your kind meddling with our destinies."

"That's why we must go to Antitis," Grimface said.

"I will never understand your kind. Wield such great powers yet are fragile as frozen branches."

Bulvife approached with a cup of wine in his hand. "Last night is only a blur to me," he said. "Do you remember anything," he addressed Benhargan.

The man turned to him, "The woman took you like she was the man, and you loved it," Benhargan laughed.

"So, you don't remember either," Bulvife said as he turned to Grimface. "Do you know what went on last night?" Chali came from the room and stood between Benhargan and Bulvife. She said nothing, but both men fell to her spell of beauty.

"Now, I will entertain you. One at a time though." She took Bulvife by the hand and he followed her like a lost lamb into the villa. Somewhere in the darkness the sounds of epic pleasure rose. For an hour this went on, then she returned Bulvife and went away with Benhargan.

Grimface ate from the table while the sounds akin to the delights of the black lotus echoed throughout. The sun came over the mountains and Chali returned Benhargan. The man looked weak, his face pale and drawn. "No mortal woman could have done such a thing. I am contented to take only mortal women from now on," he said, his eyes bulging and his legs shaking.

She laughed and ate from the table. For some time, no one spoke. The barbarians drank and ate as if having been starved. Chali and Grimface grazed. By the time the sun was above the shoreline, Grimface's sister led them to a long boat made of white wood. "We must go now." she said and smiled at Benhargan and Bulvife while pointing at the oars. "To your work, beasts."

The boat glided through the blue waters with little effort. For every draw at the oars, the craft seemed to fly over the lake. The speed of transport made Benhargan and Bulvife unsettled, yet they both kept rowing knowing that their cargo was enchanted. In due course they arrived at the far end of the lake where a wide river plunged into the dark waters. Chali directed them to put a shore and they all found footing on dry land.

"It will be five days of travel to the borders of Kom. Form there we will pass through the valley of Yamen, and to the river Styn. We can take the river to the sea, and there cross to Antitis." she said.

"How do you think we will pass through the valley of Yamen," Grimface said.

"It is the only way. The prince has sent agents to retrieve the amulet. And now that he knows we have it, he will seek to intercept us at any possible exit point." She smiled warmly, "This is the impossible exit, and he will not be guarding it."

"Why is this way impossible?" Bulvife stated.

"The valley of Yamen is where the black lotus grows in vast fields of boggy water," Grimface said. "Those who venture there are enslaved to its potent scent, and most serve the rest of their lives tending the harvest until they succumb to the flower and become food for its roots."

Benhargan took to the woods, "Stop chattering like monkeys and let's get moving." He vanished into the forest.

Bulvife waited. Chali moved into the brush as did Grimface. Bulvife took up the rear. The witch seemed at ease in the woods as she followed Benhargan's path perfectly. Grimface followed her, and he too followed the ranger with uncanny precision. Bulvife kept his bow at the ready. Benhargan was ahead and from time to time would purposely break a small twig on a sapling or bush to communicate with Bulvife. They all moved with great speed.

As night came on, they found shelter at the base of the mountain. Pines and scrubs littered the area. A circle of stones was clear of debris, and Chali led them to the center where a ring of stones lay. "We will make camp here," she said. "Tobin falls are not far from here." The sound of rushing water was plain to hear. They camped and drank from the sacred springs that bubbled up by the river. The water was bitter and filled with bubbles. "Draw your strength from this water. It will sustain you as well as manna," Chali said.

Grimface made a fire and the four of them sat around eating bread and cheese. "It is rare that anyone comes this way. In my youth there were no settlements here in the mountains and the bears and lions tested only the heartiest of our kind."

"We lost hundreds to the bear-folk and the prides," Chali said. "But things have changed since we were children. "The bear-folk are all gone, and the lion-men have moved elsewhere. Men have hunted these forests for four hundred years, and for a time they came to me and traded furs for medicine." She poked the fire with a stick, "The villagers who live on top of the mountain will help us on our quest but will not venture into Yamen. They mostly trade the sticky lotus leaf for goods."

"I don't like this. We are exposed here," Benhargan said.

"I'll keep first watch." Bulvife stated to Benhargan. "I'll wake you by false dawn."

Grimface looked up, "No. I will set a sentry to guard us. We all must sleep and save our strength." He stood and walked the edge of their camp. He began to hum, then chant, then sing. The leaves of the bushes glowed, as did the spring water and stones. Images began to appear around the camp, grotesque and deformed in a hellish red light. The light faded and the dark black creatures stood facing outward, their long tails switching back and forth. Grimface returned to the fire and collapsed. "It is done. Now, let us sleep the night." His eyes were demon like, and they closed halfway as his breathing turned to a shallow panting.

Chali came close to him and laid her hands on his chest. She spoke some strange words and Grimface's clothes glowed green then faded too normal. She sat back at the fire and again poked at it with a stick. "He will know what it means to rest this night. Now, we three must discuss preparations for crossing the Yamen valley." She took the stick and drew pictures in the air with smoke. "When we are in the first village, find me four empty wine amphorae and some hemp rope. We have an apparatus to make before we can cross the next valley." She explained her plan to the two Cimmerians while Grimface lay fast asleep.

CHAPTER 4
ZOMBIES THAT TEND THE LEAF

THE SUN WAS BLAZING down on the lake valley, but the temperature in the mountains was cool enough to support glaciers and frost in the shadows. Benhargan scaled the hill like a mountain sheep. Once at the top, he waited for the other three.

As they crested the top, a path appeared and Benhargan followed it, as did the others. They walked for miles through the high pines and exposed white granite. The path crossed a creek, its fast-moving white water rushed through the boulders and crags on its way toward the lake below. Benhargan cupped his hands and drank at the edge of the estuary. Bulvife came along side and did the same. "How many miles to that village," Benhargan said.

"Not far now," Chali stated. "When you begin to feel separated from your sense, you'll know we are close."

Bulvife looked at Benhargan and shrugged, "Strange how she knows all this."

"She's a wizard," Benhargan commented. "But don't forget that wizards don't know everything."

Grimface knelt down and drank from the water. "Be wary of the Katahe village," he gave them both a concerned look. "They send strangers to tend the black lotus. They never come back."

"I'll send some of them to tend my lotus." Benhargan grunted.

"Come, we must get moving," Bulvife stated.

They crossed the brook and headed along the trail deeper into the pinewoods. Large clumps of yellow sap clung to the trunks and branches of the green trees. In the wind was a strange sound, like voices, or whispers. By midday they had come to the edge of a large village. Round stone foundations with wooden walls and moss-covered roofs were spread out on a wide bluff overlooking a broad valley. In the air was a strange odor; pine, jasmine, lavender, cinnamon, and fresh baking bread all were terms that could be used to describe it, but it was none of those things. Bulvife looked relaxed, "The scent of the lotus," he said.

Benhargan's eyes took on a dreamy lilt, "Yes, such a fair stench, few can call it false."

"Keep your wits stupid barbarians," Grimface stated, "or, you'll be down in that valley tending the black lotus till you rot."

Chali led them through the strange people of the village. Benhargan towered above these small brown people who had dark hair and blue eyes. Bulvife shook his head a few times trying to clear the placid feeling. Grimface stopped at a tall blue-gray stone that was three times as tall as Benhargan. "Now, seek the amphorae and bring them here," he said.

Both barbarians moved out, though their steps were awkward and without care. A large panther appeared from around one of the buildings, a jeweled collar around its neck and a long brass chain leading away from it. Both Benhargan and Bulvife reacted by notching arrows, then they saw the beast's master emerge. She was not like the natives. Her skin was pale white, and long slender bare legs led to a narrow waste and shoulders. Long flowing white hair hung down to the small of her back. On her feet were moccasins, tied with leather straps up around her calves. She stopped and observed the two barbarians for a moment, then smiled showing her white teeth, "You are strangers, no?"

Bulvife just stared at her. Benhargan took in a deep breath as if he were going to say something, then also just stared. She made a bawdy laugh, pulled on the leash of her panther and strolled past the two men. Grimface watched with extreme interest as she eyed the two barbarians, then walked around one of the huts and vanished. Chali scoffed, "She's from Hem; sluts and connivers one and all."

Grimface chuckled. "I had two in my harem."

"Let's not dredge that up." Chali looked annoyed. "Let those beasts of yours find the jars, and we will manufacture the rest." She looked about, "The lotus is strong up here, stronger than I remember."

"They've had a thousand years to cultivate it and grow the garden," Grimface said.

"Of course. Let's find the leather and soft pine wood," Chali smiled. "Soon all these mortal troubles will be behind us."

"Are you sure your prophesy visions are true?" Grimface looked concerned.

Chali smiled, "As true as they ever were."

Grimface nodded. "Very well then."

Bulvife and Benhargan brought two empty wine amphorae and set them down. Saying nothing, they both turned and went searching for two more. Chali and Grimface were too busy to notice the men as each focused on their own projects. Chali worked to take long tubes of tauboo grass and wrap them in leather. Grimface found a carpenter and borrowed his chisel and knife and set to work fashioning cone shaped containers. By midday, they had finished. "Now, Cimmerians find us two long poles and some rope," Grimface ordered. He carefully took an awl and drilled two tube size holes into the amphora. He put the tubes wrapped tauboo tubes in and sealed them with pitch from a pine tree. By the time Benhargan and Bulvife returned, Chali and Grimface were done. "Secure the jars to the poles and be careful not to cause damage to the tubes," Grimface said.

The two barbarians did as they were told and soon, they had a litter that carried the four amphoras. Benhargan examined the four tubes snaking away from one jar at the end. Attached to the opposite one was a bellows. "What a strange abomination you have made Grimface," he said.

"As we walk into the valley, we must not breathe the toxic black lotus air. We will push the air through this amphora filled with oil, then it will go through this one filled with vinegar, then through this one filled with water, and finally through the last one filled with hemmet weed." He patted the amphora with the four tubes coming out of it, "Then we breathe the air that is purified." He showed the two warriors how to fix the wooden cone over their nose and mouth, then he pumped the bellows and air bubbled through coming out of the tubes.

"Smells like monkey shit," Bulvife stated.

"That's the hemmet weed," Grimface chuckled, "You'll get used to it or die a long and horrible death." He took one of the wooden masks and took a sniff, "Smells like the inside of a tomb," he added.

Chali looked angry, "You have no right to complain," she said. "It's important that we make it across the valley in one day. These filtering jars will not last more than that. We will rest here tonight and begin in the morn."

"Let's find a hut and rest for the coming exodus," Grimface stated as he moved further into the town. Many small brown natives moved about, along with others who were not native. Tall white Hemites mingled in the market with squat Torqs and Yems. Some were caravanners trading goods for dried black lotus and other' bartered for the rare herbs that grew up on the mountain. Some were working metals at forges, and other foreigners were showing materials such as silk, cotton, and gossamer. It took little time to find a hut willing to put them up for the night. All the while the smell of the raw lotus from the valley dulled their wits.

Darkness settled and the four remained in the hut while merriment and drinking was conducted outside. The yellow glow of a bonfire made shadows dance at the door, and the occasional yelp from a drunk, or drugged travelers could be heard. Benhargan took first watch and sat facing the door with his sword across his lap. By the time Bulvife took his place near the door, it was predawn. A few times he saw a strange shadow lurk near the door, linger for a moment, then vanish. *A drunk looking for an open hut*, he thought.

In the distance a hawk cried, and Grimface roused and stood. "All awake, we leave as soon as you are ready."

Bulvife and Benhargan shouldered the litter with the amphora. They started out of the village and down the mountain toward a vast swampy mire. "Put on your masks," Grimface told them. As they descended, it was evident that large black flowers floated suspended in pools of water as far as the eye could see. Intermixed were people, tending the flowers. As they got closer, a terrible sight came into view. Thousands of wandering souls, blank expressions on their faces, and dull gray eyes wandered from flower to flower. Some of them had been injured; bloody and infected wounds seeped white and yellow puss that fell into the water. Some were missing limbs, and others had raised boils. Grimface pumped the bellow constantly as they stepped into the first pool and sank up to their knees.

The water was dark only because of the reflection of the black petals of the lotus plants. Each lotus was as big as a shield and was secured to five dark green leaves that floated in the water. They pressed on. It seemed that the souls who wandered in this floral waste land were uninterested in them, and at times bumped into them only to give a dull look and then move away to another plant.

They traveled for several hours when Bulvife's muted voice rang out, "A village."

Thatch roofed; reed walled huts appeared on an island in the middle of the sea of black. More natives were about; some stacking harvested lotus leaves, and others looking at the four travelers.

"Who are you to travel across the sacred valley?" A shriveled native came toward them.

Bulvife drew his sword, "Keep your distance," he warned.

"We are merely crossing. We have no interest in the leaf," Grimface said.

"Take your masks off," the native called.

"We only wish to pass in peace," Grimface furthered.

The native raised his arms in the air and an iridescent yellow glow passed over them. He called out loudly, "Come children of the lotus, pull these sinners to paradise. Come take their masks from them." A collective moan filled the air all around them.

"Quickly," Grimface shouted. They began to run.

It was no easy task to pump the bellows and run, but Grimface did so. Behind them shambled hundreds of the tenders of the lotus, but they didn't move very fast, and soon the four had outpaced the hoard. "Slow your pace," Grimface stated, "It is safe to walk again."

"I do not like this land of stinking flowers," Benhargan said. "You should have let Bulvife, and I feed the plants with the corpse of those fools."

"They are unfortunate souls," Chali said. "Pity them rather than condemn them."

Finding a high place, they climbed from the water and stood for a moment. "How much further until we can get rid of this apparatus," Bulvife questioned.

"Another five miles, maybe ten," Chali stated. "Not far."

The mud was thick, and Benhargan complained about not killing the tenders nearly every step. Bulvife remained quiet, alert, and focused. Soon the ground angled upward, and they were out of the bogs and onto dry land again. Several more hours and they were looking down into the valley from a thousand feet up. The wind blew down the hill and Grimface took off his mask. "It's okay, the scent is not coming toward us."

It took no time for the two barbarians to set the litter aside and start loping up the mountainside. The air was fresh and moist. By the time they reached the next village, the sun was setting. A dark blood-red sky illuminated the coming darkness. Grimface sat on a large round boulder and as the sun dipped down, he chanted softly. The chant became a song and soon the eerie tune set the stones vibrating. The air bent and the sky fractured, and from the earth came a twisted man-shaped creature, a demon. Grimface stood and pointed. In a strange language he conversed with the monster, then it turned its back on him, folded its arms, and looked out toward the lotus bogs. "We can rest now with little fear." Grimface sat down as Bulvife made a fire. They ate some dried meat and drank some wine from a skin. By the time the night was failing, Chali and Grimface had settled. Bulvife took first watch.

Bulvife watched the stars moving overhead. From time to time he would peer out into the darkness to see the dark shape of the demon standing watch. He suddenly shook his head and stared intently, for he could not believe what he was seeing. A woman was approaching led by a panther on a chain. She approached the demon, whose wings extended, but she waved her hand and the thing vanished. In what seemed no time, she was standing before him, the panther sat, and she ran her hands over his hardened biceps.

"You are weary. I am told that your master bears the seal of the God King. Is this so?" She looked deep into his eyes. A darkness filled Bulvife's mind and for a moment he knew not what he was doing.

His sight returned and blood dripped from his face. A loud voice was bombarding him. On the ground was the decapitated body of the woman, and to the side the remains of the panther. Fire raged all around and the booming voice roused him. "Come with me now or die in the fire!" Benhargan shouted. His limbs came to life, and he quickly followed Benhargan up the trail.

"What happened," Bulvife said.

"You let that witch walk up on us. It was only luck that I stood to relieve my bowels as she took the amulet from Grimface. I took her hand at the wrist, but she let her panther loose, then all of the underworld broke loose."

"How did the fire start?"

Benhargan dodged a plummeting tree limb engulfed in flames. "This way," he cried leading the way up a set of boulders and toward a patch of ground void of vegetation. Standing there were Chali and Grimface, both looked beat and weary. "The woman was powerful, and it took both these wizards to undo her," Benhargan stated.

Bulvife sat down. "I don't understand what happened."

Grimface sat also, "She ruled your soft mind. You let her whisper to you, and she spoke a command that left you witless. You nearly cost us the quest," Grimface was not angry, but spoke calmly.

Chali brushed some soot off her arm. "It is no wonder, for few could resist her magic. If it wasn't for the fact that she did not get the amulet, she would have killed us all."

"It will be dawn shortly. We must make it to the port at Chikakhan by the end of this day." Grimface started climbing up the mountain.

They moved quickly. Only the wine skins had been saved from the battle. For a time, they labored up the mountain. Benhargan sped forward and led the way. Since they were no longer on the path, he took them in a semicircle to link up with the trail again. Once on the trail, they moved ever faster over the peak and down the other side. In the air was the smell of the sea, and when the trees cleared, a ruin of a city appeared, and no river could be seen.

As they got closer to Chikakahn they could see the thirty-foot-wide walls toppled, the battlements laid low, and bodies rotting in the sun as far as the eye could see. Grimface took the lead and wove his way through the field of corpses. By the time they reached the collapsed wall, it was clear that the city had been hit by a giant wave. Sea water filled the moat and ditches, fish lay baking in the sun like the bodies, and all around was seaweed and shellfish. The smell was unbelievable, and Chali gagged and vomited more than once.

In the middle of the city, they found a large rowboat on top of the temple stairs. Together, the four of them carried it to the devastated and empty docks, now only stone piers void of ships. Once in the water, Grimface and Chali sat in the middle, while Benhargan and Bulvife rowed. As they rowed out to sea Grimface looked back at the devastation. "Only the city was destroyed. Look at the land on either side, untouched for miles. Something destroyed that city."

Chali touched his arm. "A kraken," she softly said. "The prince commands it." She stood up and the wind blew her hair toward the bow. "Let us raise the sail. Rest barbarians, we will need you to have all your strength brought to bear soon."

CHAPTER 5
LOST ANTITIS

THE WATERS SMASHED against the sea cliffs with tremendous force. They were lucky not to be spotted by any naval patrols. High up on the cliffs were battlements, but the cliffs provided such an impossible approach that the walls were absent any lookouts. Benhargan sat whittling some wood with his dagger as the boat rocked high to the right, then high to the left. In the distance tidal forces came from several directions creating huge plumes of water that would spout up thirty feet into the air. In the wind was the strong smell of brimstone, and around the black broken rocks that extended into the sea, steam steadily rose. Bulvife stood near the prow, his left hand holding onto a sail rope, and his right resting on the hilt of his sword. Grimface angled the tiller and the boat shot down a trough and back up. Chali sat in the middle of the boat deep in a meditation.

"We're nearly there," Grimface said. Benhargan grunted, Bulvife nodded, and Chali did nothing.

Waves smashed into the little boat like a ram as it approached the shoreline. To his right, Grimface noticed water leaking slowly into the bottom of the boat. On the left some rope-cocking came loose high on the saxboard, and more water leaked in. The boat took another broadside and water pooled at the bottom. Chali appeared ill-concerned as water covered her legs and hips. Grimface angled the boat down a trough. Upon reaching the other side, the jagged boulders surrounded them on every side. Waves as big as a building smashed over the rocks showering the little boat with a deluge of water. Now, with the water at her shoulders Chali stood up, "The Kracken is no longer a concern for us." She climbed up on one of the stout cross bars and stood on the sideboard. Grimface wove them through several jutting rocks then angled them back toward a low depression in the cliff. Just before reaching the niche, a wave picked up the boat high into the air and dropped it onto the rocky shore. The keel snapped, all occupants were thrown clear, and the remains of the long boat were dragged back into the sea.

Benhargan grabbed Grimface, and Bulvife Chali, pulling them both from the tidal waters into the depression. Benhargan dropped Grimface to the pebbles and turned to the sea. Things were there, amongst the waves. Man like shapes stood upon the water. More appeared, and a low harmonic sound hit the two barbarians.

"They're laughing at us," Bulvife said drawing his sword.

Grimface got to his feet coughing up water. "They are," he struggled to say. "The elementals..." He coughed again, "They are the guardians of this island."

"Let them come and I will lay them low," Benhargan boasted.

Bulvife helped Chali to her feet. She stood, staggered, and Bulvife caught her. "Now what?" he said.

Grimface stepped back and looked up the cliff. "We climb." He began to move up the broken rock slowly hand over hand. No birds circled overhead, and the water elementals vanished under the waves. Higher and higher Grimface climbed until he came to a ledge not more than five hands wide. He stood with his back to the rock and looked out to sea. In the distance a row of what looked like five exposed pointed rocks appeared, then vanished below the waves. "The Kracken is awake and seeking prey." he said.

"I fear no such beast!" Bulvife shouted up. "No Cimmerian does or will!"

Benhargan chuckled as he reached the ledge. "I will deal it death and throw it back into the sea whence it came." The space became crowded. "Now what wizard," he demanded, "shall we stand here and wait for the seasons to change?"

Grimface turned with great effort and laid his hands on the rock. He sang a tune that caused the stones to vibrate, and the rocks cracked along a seam. Pushing on one side an opening appeared, dark and musty. "Inside barbarian," he pointed.

The tunnel stunk of old air and dust. The dirt below their feet was soft. Grimface knelt down and put his hand into soil. "Like peaty earth," he said while peering into the darkness.

"This was part of the old villa that dominated this place on the island. Back when the Antitis elders ruled with a triumvirate, this forgotten lair was Oland Bullveryo's palace," Grimface stated.

Chali came into the blackness. "Why have you not illuminated this place?" She spoke softly and with authority. "Make the darkness abate," she said and black iron sconces along the wall flashed with fire. The roof was void of bats, and the floor was covered in a thick black powder.

Grimface took the lead moving down the passage. Anti-chambers branched off the long tunnel. Glancing into a few portals he noticed the outlines of stone tables and benches, long forgotten metal works, and other dark doorways. Ahead he could see a set of stone stairs going up. "Stay close," he said.

The way up was long, and a few times they all stopped to catch their breath. At last, a shimmer of natural light appeared above them and they found themselves covered in green ivy at the edge of a courtyard. Remnants of wood could be seen at the edges of the stairwell, and loose iron rivets that had fallen down the stairs. Grimface turned to look down the stairwell at his companions. "Here our paths diverge barbarians. We've spent many a month together. I will be sad to see this fellowship end. Now, your path is to defeat the prince's guards, free the King, and lead his people to the docks where they must set sail before the vail of night comes. Our job," he looked into Chali's face, "is to tax the power of the prince, and battle the Kracken. We will hold them both as long as possible. Direct the ship Captains south, and don't stop for any reason until you strike land." He parted the ivy, "Now go and we shall do our best to not fail you!"

Benhargan came up and laid his meaty hand on Grimface's shoulders. "I will pray that Crom knows your worth." He moved into the courtyard.

Bulvife came up next. "I've learned much in my days at your heels. I hope that your gods give you peace once you are among your family." He looked into Chali's eyes then followed Benhargan.

"It is our time. I have the amulet. Let us make this stand and be done with it." Grimface moved across the courtyard. The verandas were empty, and no guards patrolled the colonnades. He and Chali found their way easily into the palace-fortress.

Inside, the halls were mostly empty. Only a few times they had to hide in a dark nook to avoid detection. At a wide marble stairway, he found a row of cane poles. He grabbed one as he moved up the stairs that led to the next level. Sinister sounds echoed down while they climbed stealthily upward. At the top a wide walkway led to a host of arched doorways. Grimface peaked into one. It opened out onto a wide veranda that overlooked the sea. There, in the middle of the terrace was a stone alter, long and flat. Chained to it was a young girl and standing above her a man dressed in a dark purple robe with a brass knife in his hand. Swirling dark images hovered around him, and every few moments his body shot lightning from all four limbs causing his bones to show through cloth and skin.

"It is far worse than we thought," Grimface said. "He's sacrificed to the gods, and his power is strong."

"It will be a trifle when we stand together. He cannot stop fate," she said.

BENHARGAN AND BULVIFE moved down a corridor. The sound of footsteps came toward them, and they hid in a dark alcove. The sound stopped. Bulvife removed his knife, and Benhargan couched ready to attack. The sound began again. Three armed guards passed. Benhargan looked at Bulvife and made a comical face then motioned for them to advance. Skulking from the darkness they moved down the aisle. Rectangular doorways appeared every twenty feet, and from time to time they could see slaves or soldiers milling about. Finally, a waft of fresh sea air filled Bulvife's nose. Benhargan smelled it too, and the two barbarians made for the origin of the draft. Not more than a hundred steps and they came to sunlight and open air. From their vantage a wide-open terrace met their eyes. Across from them was a large temple, the main doors were barred, and soldiers stood every ten paces surrounding it.

"That's where the King and his people are kept," Benhargan surmised.

"A frontal assault is not practical," Bulvife said. "Another entrance perhaps?" He pointed to several open windows along a continuous ledge that circled the top of the structure.

Benhargan shrugged, "Open portals, but how do we get up there, fly?" He thought for a moment. "What about that?" He pointed at another building not far away surrounded by a scaffolding complete with ropes, pulleys, and a boom. "Let's go." He moved quickly ducking down below a long stone planter that ran the length of the terrace. Bulvife followed.

Soon they were near the scaffolding. An exposed area the length of four tall men separated them from getting to the rope. Benhargan peeked around the corner. Half a dozen armed men stood near the end of the temple. Suddenly a deep voice echoed to the two barbarians.

"Anything to report?"

Benhargan looked around the corner. A Captain was engaging the guards. Benhargan looked at Bulvife, "We go now." He ran to the scaffolding and nimbly climbed the five stories to the top. Bulvife was just behind. Once at the top, the two men quickly and silently moved to the boom. A long rope was coiled up on the top platform and its end tied to the end of the boom. Behnargan took up the rope, and estimated the distance to the other wall. He prepared to leap when a deep rumbling shook the ground.

"The Kracken," shouted one of the guards.

"Shut up," chided the captain. "Leave it be and do your job!"

Benhargan looked out to sea and could see a beast of black scales, crab like arms, and octopus face reared up out of the water as high as the top of the temple. It looked toward the island, then it submerged causing a massive wave to rush toward the city. The water smashed into the island and washed over the feet of the guards. Screams from within the temple erupted. The guards looked uneasy. Benhargan leapt.

He fell through the air as the rope became taunt then he rose up to the temple ledge. Reaching out he grabbed on to a statue's arm and pulled himself up. Bulvife did the same and Benhargan latched on to him and pulled him to the edge. "Pull up the rope and bring it," he said. Bulvife pulled up the rope and cut it from the boom. "I'll lower you down to the door. You unbar it and we'll lead the souls out," Benhargan said.

Bulvife looped the rope around himself and Benhargan lowered him slowly down. The guards were standing with their back to them. At the bottom, Bulvife lifted the large wooden bar from the brackets. Once out, Benhargan hoisted him up. They both climbed down through the window into the temple. Before anyone was aware they had moved through the crowd and stood at the double doors. "When the doors open, we will kill many guards. You who are able-bodied men take up their weapons and follow us to the harbor. You, women and children, stay close as we go, for if you fall out of line, you will be lost." Benhargan turned and shoved the doors open.

The startled guards at the entrance turned and were cut down by Benhargan and Bulvife. Two men grabbed their weapons and joined the barbarians in the assault. Ten more guards fell before the mercenaries could mount a counterattack. The elite King's guard armed themselves and a slaughter fell upon the prince's soldiers. Luckily, no alarm was sounded, and Benhargan led them all down a narrow street toward the harbor.

GRIMFACE MOUNTED THE amulet on the pole. "It is time," he said as he stepped out into the doorway. He raised the amulet and began to sing. The prince turned, his eyes bulging with insane rage. "You," the prince shouted. "I command the pearl of Atlantis and you shall not stand in my way!" He raised his hands and blue lightning shot from his hands encapsulating Grimface.

Slowly the blue abated as flames erupted all around. A shockwave emanated cracking stone and felling statues. The prince toppled from the alter. He scrambled to his feet and shook his head, "You'll have to do better than that." Running to a planter, he pulled forth a box and set it on the dais. Opening it he gasped.

"No more do you have it," Chali shouted, in her hand a white pearl the size of a catapult stone. She concentrated, and the pearl glowed a bright white. Creatures appeared all around, iridescent white beings with gold wings. They flew toward the prince, and he raised his hands.

A wall of black appeared for a second and the white creatures were gone. "The pearl was mine; do you not think that I know its secrets!" The prince narrowed his gaze at Chali. She screamed as her skin withered. The pearl fell to the ground, then the prince cried out in pain. A lance of fire pierced his middle and he fell to his knees.

Grimface approached, in his hand the staff. "I consign you to oblivion, to writhe in pain at the mercy of your victims," he said as spectral arms lurched from the stone floor and grasped the prince. They clawed at his flesh tearing chunks from his bones. He struggled, cried in anguish as his soul was rendered, and his body burnt to ash. Chali stood up and took up the pearl. She ran to the balcony and stood there singing. The Kracken came and rose out of the sea. The ground shook several times and fire shot from the ground around them.

BENHARGAN FOUND THE galleys still moored at the harbor. The King's people rushed aboard each. Sailors quickly found their stations and the ropes were cut. The boats lurched out into the harbor and toward the breakwater. Bulvife turned to see the Kracken standing as docile as a bear cub near the palace. Lava was dripping down the sides of the cliffs making waterfalls of fire. On the ledge he could see a single person, a glowing orb in her hand. "It's Chali," he shouted to Benhargan.

THE GROUND FRACTURED and shifted upward. "Use the amulet to hold back the volcano." Chali called. Grimface raised the staff and sang for all he was worth. His nerves were a blaze with the magic, and he concentrated on binding the land. Lava poured out from fishers, smoke and gasses filled the air. All the while the Kracken stared at Chali and the pearl. Grimface could feel his strength being tested. In his vision he could see Chali there. This would be it, the last of their kind lost with the end of this island. She glanced back and smiled at him. He focused all the more.

"Not much longer now," she said.

THE GALLEY MADE IT out to sea and away for Anita's. For hours the rowers toiled. The island became further and further away until only the smoke from the volcano could be seen. A man in his forties came and stood by the railing. He looked out at where the island was. "All lost," he shook his head in despair. He turned to Benhargan and Bulvife, "You saved my people. I should reward you, but now I have nothing. What would you have of me brave warriors?"

Benhargan looked the man up and down. Clearly, he was the old King. "All that I ask is that you make a villa when you settle again. In that villa you will put a statue of the man and woman who truly saved you. Servants will tend those statues and sacrifice daily of food and wine," he said.

"As you will it, it shall be done." The King looked back at the horizon. A trickle of gray smoke was visible.

GRIMFACE COULD NO LONGER hold back the forces of nature. The amulet was designed to make a change in nature then let nature take its course; he knew it was only a matter of a few minutes until his strength failed. The Kracken suddenly turned and vanished below the rim of the balcony. Chali turned and held the pearl out. Grimface found himself surrounded by a bright light. She nodded to him, and he collapsed to the floor. Everything around them turned red and white, black and gray. Death was now here. Darkness fell upon him like a wet wool blanket.

IN THE DISTANCE A FLASH appeared. A column of smoke, thick and dark rose into the air forming a mushroom cloud. A rumble came over the water followed by a rush of hot air stinking of brimstone. All that were on the deck of the galley were forced to the wooden planks. The water rose high, and the vessels of the King began moving very fast. Women screamed, children cried, and men prayed as the boats picked up speed. In the distance a mass of land appeared, growing larger by the minute. "Hold on," Bulvife said as they met the shore and flowed inland with the wave. The ship passed above palm trees and went over large rocks, and finally bumped into a hill. It swirled around several times, then landed hard and tilted to the side as the water rushed away. The devastation was vast. Trees were laid out like fallen spears and the King's people filtered out of the boats onto soggy land. A rain of rocks began to fall as the sky turned black, and darker than any moonless night.

Hours passed as debris fell piling up around the boats. The air was choked with stinking sulfur and thick with ash. They all sheltered on the lee side of the boat until the ash and rock piled up around them. A boom in the distance echoed and rain began to fall. For hours the water fell from the sky. From time-to-time fish hit the ground as did seaweed and shellfish. The terrified people stayed huddled waiting for this nightmare to end.

HE GASPED FOR AIR. A chunk of wood poked at him. Pulling himself up, Grimface looked around. Where was he? He didn't know. Some cruel joke must have been played on him. This place didn't look like his home in the afterlife. Then he coughed out a chuckle. *Of course, the village is at the bottom of a lake now*, he thought. Slowly he began paddling with his arms. In the distance he heard waves breaking on a shore. *There are no waves like this on a lake*, he thought. In his head he heard a voice. "I could not let you fall with me," Chali's voice was clear as a bell. "Forgive me brother for my deceit, but you would not have helped if you knew that I was to be a sacrifice."

Tears welled up in his eyes as Grimface cried out, "It is not as it should be!" He climbed up on the board, "Why... why would you do this thing?"

"It is not for you to decide when to die. The gods decide that. Look to the west, when the blue star falls to the earth. There you will find your place, and all will be revealed to you. Until then, know that my love was too great to stay, and too weak to let you go."

An unsettling quiet fell over him. The board began to plummet toward a yellow sandy shore. He hit hard and rolled over and over in the waves that slammed against the beach. He clawed his way up toward a barren plateau. In the distance he could see some white smoke. Getting to his feet, he shambled toward the smoke.

The amulet of the God-King was gone now. What would he do next? As his sister said, it was not for him to choose. Stopping, he brushed off his torn shirt and breeches. He stood to his full height and took in a deep breath. "I hope they have wine," he said. Leveling his gaze at the smoke, he again began walking that way.

Don't miss out!

Visit the website below and you can sign up to receive emails whenever Lawrence BoarerPitchford publishes a new book. There's no charge and no obligation.

https://books2read.com/r/B-A-MRTR-RKVVB

BOOKS 2 READ

Connecting independent readers to independent writers.